A Candlelight Ecstasy Romance®

HE CAUGHT HER EASILY AND LOWERED HER SLOWLY TO THE GROUND.

She was aware of every square inch of her uncovered back as she stood cradled against his chest. Silently, calmly, she counted one, two, three buttons on his linen shirt. His hands slid from the sides of her waist to her belly, and his flat palms, fingers spread, moved slowly up and down the vee formed by her thighs and torso.

"So I was wrong," he murmured. "You are strong enough." His hands slid lightly up the fabric of her dress across her midriff.

Her last deep breath had become almost a moan as Leda whispered, "Nat . . . hold me." He knew without asking what her simple request meant.

Leda shuddered under wave after wave of novel, surging desire. It was all so . . . new. "Nat," she moaned softly. "Please . . . more."

"Ah, Leda . . . more . . . is what there is . . . More . . ." He turned her toward him, trailing his lips in a scorching line along the curve of her shoulder. "And more . . . Oh, darlin', and still more . . ."

TROUBLE IN PARADISE

Antoinette Hale

A CANDLELIGHT ECSTASY ROMANCE®

Published by
Dell Publishing Co., Inc.
1 Dag Hammarskjold Plaza
New York, New York 10017

Dell ® TM 681510, Dell Publishing Co., Inc.
Candlelight Ecstasy Romance®, 1,203,540, is a registered
trademark of Dell Publishing Co., Inc., New York, New York.

ISBN: 0-440-19078-9

Printed in the United States of America
First printing—April 1984

To Peg, Tom, Sharon—and John.

To Our Readers:

We have been delighted with your enthusiastic response to Candlelight Ecstasy Romances®, and we thank you for the interest you have shown in this exciting series.

In the upcoming months we will continue to present the distinctive sensuous love stories you have come to expect only from Ecstasy. We look forward to bringing you many more books from your favorite authors and also the very finest work from new authors of contemporary romantic fiction.

As always, we are striving to present the unique, absorbing love stories that you enjoy most—books that are more than ordinary romance.

Your suggestions and comments are always welcome. Please write to us at the address below.

Sincerely,

The Editors
Candlelight Romances
1 Dag Hammarskjold Plaza
New York, New York 10017

CHAPTER ONE

She was lost—on an island two miles wide and five miles long. "That," she told herself, "takes more than average imagination."

The temperature in the car was at about 350° Fahrenheit and Leda Sayers was feeling moderately cooked. A thermometer inside her head seemed to be throbbing "done, done, done," and funny little black spots flitted back and forth in front of her. Heatstroke could not be far behind.

She turned off the ignition and inhaled deeply. *Calm down, take it easy, this is the Caribbean, after all. People don't get upset in Paradise.*

Leda got out and morosely surveyed the scene. One lane and impassable ahead. Which meant backing the car down, half a mile at least, to rejoin the main road of the dry, scrubby island. With both hands, she held her long golden hair up away from her neck. For a good strong hair clip, she'd cheerfully have given all the money in her purse. For a cotton sun dress, she'd consider throwing in her soul. She owned hair clips and sun dresses, of course, but they were in her luggage, and her luggage was lost somewhere between icy Boston and sunny Bequia. That left her with the gray woolen suit she was wearing—chic, elegant, and scratchy.

Summoning what was left of her willpower, Leda forced herself back behind the wheel and turned the key. Nothing happened. Alarmed, she turned it again. Not a cough, not a wheeze. Like an ancient and gentle creature, the old Chevrolet had died quietly during its nap.

Leda climbed back out, kicked a tire irrationally, and set off for the main road on foot. Five hours late so far. For a trip that required the combined services of a bus driver, two airline pilots, a taxicab driver, and a ferryboat captain, not all that bad. But would her new boss be equally philosophical?

The lane was evenly divided between rocks and potholes—an interesting challenge for the mule-footed, perhaps; but Leda was wearing two-inch leather heels. From somewhere the sound of ocean surf penetrated her misery. Surf meant sand, and on sand it was possible, even enjoyable, to walk.

That ocean is around here someplace. It's blue and refreshing and wet. I know I'd recognize it if I saw it.

Plunging into a nearly overrun footpath that led through thick brush, Leda made her way toward the gentle sound of the surf. A bramble took a swipe at her cheek, missed, and settled instead for her new silk blouse, opening a triangular tear in it.

"That does it!" The omens simply were not favorable. To have sold her furniture and car and boarded the cat, all for a job in a hostile climate? It was time to go back. Or, should she be stubborn about it? From somewhere nearby, the ocean murmured soothingly, *Find me if you can.* She tucked her long, straight hair behind her ears. What the heck; the first two thousand miles were usually the hardest.

After some tricky maneuvering, Leda emerged at last onto a strip of pure white sand, absolutely pristine and entirely deserted. Serene loveliness lapped softly at the shoreline. From the palest of blues, the ocean deepened into a vivid aquamarine and finally into a brilliant blue, the cobalt blue of hopelessly amateurish paintings. Far out, a murky reef shaded brown and gold, dividing shoal water from deep.

A wide smile lit her face. "Bingo!" Impulsively she kicked off her high-heeled shoes and waded ankle-deep into the water; it was irresistibly warm. Leda looked around guiltily. Maybe a quick swim? There were no houses, no sign of life anywhere. In less than sixty seconds all her clothes lay folded on the sand and Leda was in the water, swimming away from shore with a lazy breaststroke, cooling down her overheated body.

Her long, athletic limbs reveled in the chance to stretch and

12

twist and slip completely unhindered through the warm, buoyant water. She dove far down, and when her lungs felt ready to explode, she reversed and climbed and burst into the sunlight, happy as a dolphin.

"Bequia, my apologies," she said, laughing. "We'll get along just fine."

Hardly a contest, when the alternative was a New England winter just beginning to flex its muscles—and a New England town too small to hold both Jeffrey and her. Darn Jeffrey. She couldn't live with him, and she wasn't sure she could live without him. They said "opposites attract," but it hadn't worked out that way.

He loved late parties, she loved Agatha Christie. It drove her crazy that he didn't have to work, and it drove him crazy that she did. He was a slave to status, fonder of his Porsche than his Labrador retriever, even. She was oblivious to such trappings and puttered around in blue jeans and a beat-up Buick. He was an indoor man; she was an outdoor woman. But Jeffrey and Leda both adored Woody Allen and country auctions, and that was part of the problem: In general they shared just enough to have made her think she'd loved him. But if that was really true, then why hadn't she stuck with him after she found out about those other . . .

She stroked steadily toward the reef. Except for the fact that he just couldn't say no to women, there was nothing actually *wrong* with Jeffrey. He was extremely nice-looking, generous to a fault, a member in good standing of every Society-to-Preserve-Something-or-Other in Newport. He knew at least three separate facts about every subject in the world; she'd always envied his glibness. But he was just so . . . picky.

She paused and floated on her back, eyes closed, arms out, legs angled toward the ocean floor. It was a moment of crystal-clear revelation. Jeffrey didn't want *her*. He wanted a cross between Eleanor Roosevelt and Jacqueline Kennedy Onassis. Leda could never be either; maybe that was why she'd immersed herself more and more in her work. Managing a yacht charter service in crazy, crowded Newport Harbor in little

Rhode Island had been absorbing and challenging. But Newport was a small town, and she kept running into Jeffrey everywhere. He was a constant reminder that she'd been a naïve fool, and she'd begun to yearn for distance between them. It wasn't likely that she'd ever run into him at Coco's Yacht Charter Service on Bequia.

Coco's! If she didn't show up there soon, Julie Simpson would be sending out a search party. It seemed suddenly farcical to Leda that she had dressed with such care and sophistication in the predawn hours in Newport that morning. Now her suit was wrinkled, her blouse torn, her hair wet, her makeup washed away—and she couldn't care less. All that mattered was to feel cool at last. . . .

The sound of an outboard motor rapidly approaching brought Leda crashing out of her misty daydream. Flopping back onto her stomach, she watched wide-eyed and appalled as a small flat-bottom boat roared up to her. Her mind said *move,* but her body said *can't.* She was nearly out to the murky reef, and the shore suddenly seemed impossibly far away. Oh, Lord.

The man at the helm of the runabout brought it to a sudden stop a few feet from Leda, cut the motor, and stood up. From Leda's position in the water he looked between eight and nine feet tall. Black beard, black hair tumbling over impossibly blue eyes. Deep tan. No shirt, khaki shorts, a bulky diver's wristwatch on his right arm. That summed up the man but not his voice. It was strong, resonant, British—and furious.

"What the *hell* do you think you're doing by the reef, you fool?" His outrage could be heard easily on the other side of the island. "Are you out of your *mind,* woman? Of all the dumb tourist . . ."

Leda blinked up at him, treading water—physically and mentally. Well, this was nice. He must be the local welcome wagon.

"I'm sorry, I . . ." she began automatically. But she wasn't certain what to be sorry *for.* More treading.

The black-haired giant leaned forward and folded his solidly muscled arms over the bow rail of his runabout. For an intermi-

14

nable moment, he watched her with a look that hovered between menace and anger.

Better head that look off at the pass, girl. "Look, whoever you are, I wasn't bothering a soul, and I'd appreciate it if you'd just . . . buzz off," she finished unimpressively.

The black brows drew back together. *Definitely menace.* "You haven't been in Bequia long, have you? Or you'd certainly know better."

Oh, cripes. There was a law against nude swimming. He must be a bobby or a gendarme or whatever they called their enforcers down here.

"You're not a . . . police officer, are you?"

"Good God, do I look like one? You *are* a fool. Or a royal innocent. Seems to me that you need looking after, either way. Get in the boat," he said evenly.

"I will *not.*" Leda spoke before she had time to think, but the idea that she would climb naked into a boat with a practically naked and very powerful-looking stranger struck her as pretty comic.

"Look, just leave me alone. Just . . . get out of here, please." A slow bubble of panic began choking off her breath. What if she should develop a cramp? She needed to rest somewhere, and soon. She stole a longing glance at the reef.

He read her look perfectly. "Were you aware that the Bequians use that reef as a dumping ground?"

Leda said nothing. She was focusing every nerve, every muscle, on her effort not to panic and drown with no clothes on.

"That reef is crawling with shark and barracuda, and I do believe it's their teatime. You're not all that meaty for a main course, but you'd make a tasty snack." His British accent clipped each word precisely: "Get . . . in . . . the boat."

A tasty snack. Ha. *For whom,* she wondered cynically. She did not like the man's look, and his arrogant, condescending tone infuriated her. And she didn't for a minute believe his scare tactic about the reef. She'd swum all her life and had never yet run into a shark.

"Thanks for the tip," she threw back at him. With the last of her energy, she began to swim directly for the reef with tired, uneven strokes. It was obviously not the response he'd expected.

"Bloody *hell* you will!" he bellowed, in a real rage now. Leda heard the outboard motor start up, and in seconds the boat was blocking her path.

No hesitation in his look this time. It was black, as black as his windswept hair. Leda felt both of her shoulders caught in a bear-trap grip as he prepared to haul her over the side of his boat. "Mermaid or tuna, it's all the same to me," he growled.

"No. *No!*" she nearly shrieked. "I'll get in. Only . . . I'm not . . . fully . . . look, would you *mind?*" And with a furious wave, she gestured that he turn away from her.

"Lady, you're not even *partly*," he said amiably, letting go of his grip. With an elaborate flourish he resumed his seat at the steering wheel, his back to her. "There's a boarding step on the transom; climb over the stern," he ordered.

For a luxurious moment Leda clung to the side rail, breathing heavily from her unsuccessful effort to escape. She was too winded to try another.

"Now."

"I'm coming, I'm coming," she returned irritably. Strong and athletic as she was, she was barely able to reach the step and collapse into the cockpit. Out of the fire, into the frying pan.

"Safely landed?" he asked casually, without looking around. She might have been a speared marlin, for all he cared.

"Of course," she replied in a breathless voice that she hoped sounded haughty.

He pointed to some long, dark, slithering shadows in the water. "Ah, the local gentry. Shall I tell them Madame will not be receiving callers today?"

Shocked and repelled, Leda stared at their quick, darting movements through the water. "What are they?"

" 'Cuda," he answered. "Actually, barracuda aren't normally a threat," he admitted. "On the other hand, they *are* extremely curious, and if a swimmer is wearing a shiny bit of jewelry—as I

16

notice you are—a 'cuda, just for fun, might be tempted to lunge at it."

Leda's hand automatically reached down to touch her gold ankle bracelet, and she felt a belated rush of very real danger. It also occurred to her that the water must be very clear indeed. Hot adrenaline tingled her cheeks, washed over her breasts, and raced down to her feet.

"I suppose I ought to thank you," she mumbled confusedly. Apology or gratitude, both seemed to come equally hard. She rubbed her arms where he had gripped them. Faint fingermarks still showed, and Leda stared at them in unthinking fascination. She resented the slight bruise, a reminder that she was beholden to this superior, arrogant creature.

"I'm curious," he said mildly over his shoulder as he brought the boat toward shore. "Why did you try to swim away? Trying to avoid a Fate Worse Than Death?"

"That's good for starters," she snapped. "I just wanted someplace to stop and rest a bit," she explained sullenly.

"Standing on fire coral? The sting isn't pleasant and the welts are worse. And, of course, breathing would be damned awkward, since the reef lies six feet below sea level."

Leda glared at his tanned and rippling back. She had an overwhelming urge to stick out her tongue, and it astonished her. How long had she known him? Ten minutes? And yet during nine of them he had handled her like an untrained puppy that had slipped its leash.

They were closing slowly with the shore, and Leda suppressed a shiver. If only she had her clothes; psychologically, they would wear like a suit of armor. Failing that, a baseball bat would be nice.

"By the way, would you like my shirt?" he asked, suddenly clairvoyant.

Leda sat upright. Had she been moaning aloud? Of course not. He was unnerving her, that was all.

"If it's no bother, yes, please," she said formally. "I feel a chill."

"That's not surprising," he said as he reached under the console for the shirt and tossed it over his shoulder at her. "You're probably starting to feel some sunburn."

"In half an hour?" She wasted a fierce look of contempt on his broad back.

"In half an hour."

"Let me guess. I've been rescued by a famous ichthyologist whose tastes in light reading"—she pulled his T-shirt over her head—"run to the *Merck Medical Manual,*" she concluded in a muffled voice. The shirt smelled entirely different from her own clothes, intensely, disturbingly male. She felt armored not in the least by it.

"Nope. I'm just an ordinary sailor with the recommended daily allowance of common sense. And something tells me, my little angelfish, that if I had just a touch more of it, I'd dump you directly on that reef without looking back."

Leda could see her own little pile of clothes on the white sand as he swung the boat around and backed it expertly toward the beach. He put the motor in neutral and turned at last to face her. A funny little smile softened the lines of his face.

"You can keep the shirt," he said in an oddly controlled voice.

"Oh, no, I couldn't . . ."

Why did it seem to her that a broad grin was aching to split his composure? His black mustache and beard accented high cheekbones, and framed a maddening, mischievous mouth. There was a dimple under that beard somewhere, she was convinced. Good grief, why was she even speculating? And those tiny white lines at the corners of his eyes—squint or laugh lines? She hoped, laugh lines. *Now stop that, girl.*

Leda stood up cautiously. The gaily printed T-shirt hung to mid-thigh; the shoulders fell midway down her upper arm. The soft material rasped against her sensitive breasts like burlap.

He swept her with an undisguised look of appreciation. "You have lovely eyes," he offered incongruously. "I'd say eight to ten feet."

Leda stared at him blankly. "Eight to ten . . . feet?"

18

"That pale green; it's the color of Caribbean water at about that depth," he observed with scientific gallantry.

And your eyes are fathomless, my friend. It was time to make her bows and back away smiling.

"Thank you again, Mr. . . ."

"Hardy. Nat Hardy. And you are?"

"Leda."

He raised an eyebrow inquisitively.

"Sayers. Well, I'd better be getting back to the . . . to the . . ." *Oh, boy.* What with all the fun she'd been having, she'd forgotten all about the little engine that couldn't. "Oh. I . . . ah . . . have a problem with the car I'm driving. It doesn't start when I turn the key." So much for graceful exits. At any other time of her life she'd have walked over hot coals rather than ask a man like him to help her. But walking over hot coals is exactly what that walk to the main road would feel like, and she was aching and exhausted. "I wonder, would you have a moment?" she barely whispered.

He glanced at his watch. "I think so," he said. "Where's the car?"

Leda recoiled from his distant politeness. "I'm sorry. You've been kind enough." Kind enough! Was that her voice? What had he done but embarrass her and ruin her day? Damn him!

"No bother," he said coolly. "But I have to be in Kingstown in St. Vincent by five-thirty."

"Well . . . if you're sure. Can I . . . ah . . . have a moment to—" she began.

"—slip into something a little more comfortable? I suppose so," he sighed.

"I'll meet you on the road," she said, all gratitude evaporated. Leda scrambled into her clothes, ran a comb quickly through her wet, tangled hair, and ducked into the brambly path. He was standing just inside, holding back the first low branch for her, and she jumped at his nearness. The pungent smell of the wild brush, her own ocean saltiness, and his husky maleness combined to assault her senses with their erotic imme-

19

diacy. He might have been Adam to her Eve. Or at the very least the Gamekeeper to her Lady Chatterley.

An ironic smile curved the corners of his lips. "You know, you *do* look rather smashing in clothes."

"Oh, these old rags?" she demurred. "You ought to see me in gum boots and a down parka." And was he suggesting that she looked better *in* than *out* of clothes, by any chance?

Leda pushed aside a bramble and yelped as she pricked her finger on a thorn.

"Here—fall in behind me," he commanded, holding back the offending branch for her. "A pity I haven't my machete with me. We could hack through this in no time."

She looked up at him quickly. Joke? No joke. His expression was tranquil and apparently not deranged. She wondered how it would all play back home in Bangor, Maine: *Dear Sis, Today I asked an ax murderer to help me start my car. That's because he'd already saved me from the sharks when I went swimming wearing only my ankle bracelet, and he seemed like a very nice person.*

The very nice person just then was standing extremely close, the length of his arm barely touching hers. Black curly hairs sizzled against soft golden fuzz; if he were formed of fire coral she could not have felt the contact more.

Leda pilfered quick looks at his Roman profile—at the clean, unbroken line of nose and forehead, and the closely trimmed, full beard. He seemed to have wandered into her life from another century; he was too big, too strong, too independent for this tiny island in this diminished age.

His thick black lashes, longer than her own, were lowered as he looked around unsuccessfully for an alternate route. "You really crawled out from there?" he asked in cheerful wonder.

"I suppose it does test the bounds of human logic," she retorted. "After you." At least she would spare herself the humiliation of having him follow her on all fours.

"Who says chivalry is dead?" he quipped. Falling gracefully onto his hands and feet, he made his way quickly through the overrun section.

Leda followed reluctantly. *Lord, just let me never see this man again,* she prayed. Life was too short to be reminded of this idiotic episode the next time she'd see his face. Then she surprised herself with a smile; she'd always been a sucker for burlesque.

He had raised himself back up to his full six feet and then some, and as Leda emerged from the tunnel of brambles, offered her his hand. He pulled her up to him, his mouth twisting into a slow, wry smile, a curious echo of her own.

"Having fun?" he asked softly.

Instantly wary, Leda tried to slip her hands from his grip, but he held them with just enough force to make freeing herself an act of melodrama. Her heart began to hammer. She stared hypnotically at his upper lip. Not for anything would she swim in those ocean eyes. "I think I'm on the verge of hysteria. It's been a long day." Would the implied threat encourage him to let her go? She held her breath. It would not.

Hardy's voice dropped to a husky register she hadn't suspected he possessed. *"Why* are you such a prickly little sea urchin?" he whispered soothingly. "Don't be distressed . . . this is the land of enchantment; no evil forces allowed." His voice was a seductive caress as he brought his face close to hers.

Sliding her wrists behind her hips, he molded her body harmoniously beneath him, and his mouth, warm and exploring, lighted on hers. A wave of surprise washed over her—the strangeness of him, the island, and the situation. She had wanted, stupidly, to say "Oh!" He took advantage of the parting of her lips; his tongue probed and teased, taunting and questioning.

He knows his mouth is delicious, was the only thought that took the trouble to form itself in her mind. All else was a rush and tumble of electrifying response. The thin silk of her blouse was absolutely no protection from the furry hardness of his chest as he pressed her to him, and Leda's sun-warmed breasts swelled with the contact. Her knees turned to jelly, her breath came short, and she felt as though a crystal wedge had been driven between her body and her reason.

21

In an almost surprised voice he drawled, "Hmmn, nice." He kissed her eyelid softly, then her hair; and then he murmured, between kisses, "Leda, tell me why you made up that remarkably dumb fiction about a disabled car."

From the back of her mind a tiny meteorite hurtled through voluptuous dizziness into clear-eyed thought. "Fiction? *Dumb* fiction!" She tore her hands so sharply from his grip that the right one became free and flew up at his face, all in one fluid reflex.

"N'uh-uh," he protested as he caught her wrist easily, "no *hitting* allowed in the land of enchantment either."

She froze, horrified at her maiden attempt at violence. "I've never, *ever*—"

"—kissed a man like that? On behalf of wives and sweethearts everywhere in the free world, hoo-ray!"

She was being defused by a skilled demolitions expert, and she was helpless to do anything about it.

With a smile of perfectly blended friendliness and contrition, he dropped a gentle kiss on the pulse of her wrist and released it. "I won't insist that you're beautiful when you're angry; as a matter of fact, you scared the hell out of me. I've never been belted by a woman before."

"I've never been called a liar before," she answered stiffly.

"Oh, now, *liar* is a bit strong. Look, Leda, I can see the car from here. It's Thomas Williams's old clunker and it runs perfectly," he said kindly, "believe it or not."

"Well, it isn't running *now,*" she hissed.

"Want to bet?" His smile was angelic.

"Name it," she challenged hotly. His confidence really was insufferable.

"Dinner tomorrow night," he said promptly. "And if the question isn't too technical," he said as they stopped at the car, "would you mind telling me how you managed to drive the car this far down the lane?"

Leda closed her eyes and took a deep breath. She must remember that he was her only hope for getting the car started. "I

22

just . . . got lost. Then the car wouldn't start. I was going for help when . . ." She broke off.

"When I fell upon you floating naked in the water?"

One more try. "Well, that was because the road was such hard going . . ."

". . . that you took the easy way and crawled through the bushes? Makes sense," he said blandly.

"It's absolutely none of your business," she snapped. "Now, can you get this thing started or not?"

"Dinner?"

She compressed her lips tightly.

"Well, of course, if you're not interested in negotiating . . ." He shrugged.

"All *right*, damn it."

He got into the car and held out an open palm. "Keys."

Leda fumbled through her handbag in a flustered search. A pair of nylons slithered out, along with his T-shirt, which she had rolled into a ball and jammed on top of them. *Watch this perfect imitation of a scatterbrained female,* she moaned to herself. Her hands felt frozen and inept. Her eyes would not distinguish the car keys from the confusion of her own keys, lipstick, compact, comb, airline schedules, pencils, and notebook; the bottom of her bag was a jumbled, interlocking mess. After a search that seemed to her to last half an hour, she produced a ring of two keys. *"Here."* She practically threw them at him.

He inserted the key and turned the ignition. The engine caught immediately.

"Not possible," she breathed.

"What time shall I pick you up?" he asked politely, getting out of the purring, deceitful machine. Obviously it was a relation of his.

"I feel like a complete . . . *fool,*" she wailed.

"Eight o'clock at Coco's?"

"I just don't understand how . . . Wait a minute. How do you know I'm staying at Coco's?" Her green eyes narrowed suspiciously. *And don't stand so near me.*

"Oh darlin'! I know heaps more than that. I know you're on

23

your way to report to Julie Simpson as manager of Coco's Yacht Charter Service. I know you missed the regular ferry from St. Vincent to Bequia, and that as a result Thomas, who was to have met you here, left you his car instead."

"And *how* do you know that?" she interrupted.

"Elementary, my dear Sayers," he said, grinning. "Bequia is a very, very small island. But I'm not finished yet. I know that you're twenty-six, single, a graduate of Brown University with a major in American Civilization—a contradiction in terms, take it from an Englishman—and you're my new boss."

Hardy was leaning against the car, arms folded across his chest. He hadn't moved a centimeter; so why did she feel she'd just been leveled by a two-by-four? "Just an ordinary sailor," he'd said. That meant . . . that meant he sailed, of course. A boat. A yacht. A yacht for charter.

He saw the illumination on her face. "You've got it. One of the boats for which you'll arrange charters is the *Swan,* a fifty-foot fiberglass ketch. Sleeps six in three cabins; two showers; gourmet cuisine. Scuba gear available, licensed instructor aboard," he rattled off in the tones of a charter brochure.

"And you're . . . skipper of the *Swan?*"

"At your service, occasionally. We'll have to talk about that over dinner tomorrow. And for heaven's sake, try to wear," he said pleasantly, "something more rational than that."

She curbed an impulse to knock off his head and got in the car. "Oh, your T-shirt," she said coolly, holding it as though it were a dead toad.

"I said it was a gift; anyway, it would never hang the same again on me," he fired, closing the door after her.

"A *very* cheap shot," Leda growled without looking at him as she threw the car into reverse. Nothing would have given her greater pleasure than to leave him in a choking cloud of dust as she roared away, Ferrari-style. But a Ferrari the Chevy was not, and the road was too rutted to allow for any kind of speed. And, of course, she was in reverse gear. Bumpety-bump, bumpety-bump, she plodded, forced to endure the sight of him

24

standing tall and easily in the middle of the road, one hand hooked through a belt loop, the other waving bye-bye. Cute.

Rotten brute! Leda's intense mortification began to fade once she'd passed the first curve and he'd dropped from her view; but a steady welling of anger bubbled up and quickly reached flash point. It occurred to her that if he were in the car now, she'd gladly run it full speed into a palm tree, taking him down with her. He was very possibly the most offensive man she'd ever met. First round to you, *Cap*-tain Hardy.

For the first time she noticed the printing on his T-shirt, which she'd flung across the front seat. Ah, yes. Every island popped out its own version for tourists. The first one she'd ever seen was from the Bahamas. This one said, "It's Better in Bequia." She remembered the oddly controlled look on his face as she stood in his boat dripping wet, wearing a T-shirt, *his* T-shirt, which said, "It's Better in Bequia." Wonderful.

If erasing that afternoon meant giving up a year of her life, she'd toss it to the winds without a second thought. Once the captain's hilarious account of the day's events made the rounds of the bars, every charter captain on Bequia would know that the new girl on the island was sex-crazed, not too bright, not too truthful, and not too mechanically inclined. *Aaaggh. And all because of my own impulsiveness and some impossibly hand-some . . . wise guy.* She flamed again in recollection of his pre-sumptuous kiss. Under other circumstances she would have hauled him into court on charges of assault. But fairness forced her to admit that her behavior would have seemed provocative and inviting to most men. A judge no doubt would have labeled her manner "inflammatory." Especially to someone as appar-ently inflammable as Captain Hardy.

In Newport she'd become convinced that yacht captains were bred for arrogance and hot tempers. Nearly every day one of them threw a tantrum or balked at some charter arrangement. Name it, and they'd object to it: kids, smokers, cats, dogs, young people, old people. But by a mixture of teasing, cajoling, and occasionally pouting, Leda had gotten the job done and kept things on a friendly but businesslike level—which wasn't easy, since yacht captains were also bred, she'd decided, for amorousness.

Damn Hardy, anyway. He'd taken a sledgehammer to the delicate balance between charter broker and yacht captain. No, it was impossible—she'd never be able to work with him now. One of them would have to go. She brightened. Perhaps he didn't mean to stay on in Bequia? Crewed charter boats were notoriously nomadic. The Caribbean this year, the South Pacific the next. It depended on the whim of the actual owner, and the hired skipper was usually a gypsy who was more than happy to oblige. Captain Hardy looked nomadic enough. But he didn't, somehow, appear the type to oblige an owner, or a guest, *or* a charter broker—if he didn't feel like it.

A quiet little sign pointed matter-of-factly to Coco's, and before long, Leda found herself approaching the wide porch of a large white clapboard house buried under a profusion of flowers. Reeling from the heady fragrance of the frangipani bushes, she crossed nervously into the lobby, a pleasant room with floor-to-ceiling French windows that allowed a gentle breeze to pass over the three or four guests having cocktails inside. She walked up to the wainscoted desk and identified herself to the black-skinned girl behind it.

Clearly the girl, a young teenager, thought Leda was an escaped felon impersonating the real Leda Sayers. "Miz Sayers, is dat?" she challenged suspiciously in her musical accent.

"Yes, I've flown from Boston and my luggage was lost and . . . is Julie Simpson in?"

"Yes, Miz Simpson wid some de guests, havin' sundowners," the young girl explained.

"I wonder if you would tell her that I've arrived."

The girl gave Leda one last incredulous look, shook her head, said, "I s'pose," philosophically, and left the room.

One nice thing, Leda mused wearily. She'd made every blooper in the book today; things could only go up from here. And they did, beginning with the entrance of Julie Simpson, one of those angels of mankind who never walked, always wafted, across a room. Tall, gray-haired, and obviously cultivated, she beamed in on Leda with a disarming smile.

"Hello hello! Our Leda at last. How nice to meet you, child. Thelma told me about your lost luggage; never fear, they always show up by the next morning. But you look exhausted, you poor thing. What time did you get up today?" she asked, all without pausing for a breath.

"Well, four o'clock this morning, I'm afraid." Or was that yesterday morning?

"And you must be famished! I was just sitting down to an early dinner with several of our guests. Would you care to join us? Or perhaps not," she decided quickly after seeing the look of panic on Leda's face. "Let me show you to your cottage. Then I'll have something sent up on a tray. A nice shower, a good night's sleep, and you'll be like new."

"I'll take it," Leda smiled gratefully, and fell in behind her employer as she led the way up a wooden step path behind the main guest house. The side of the hill was dotted with tiny cottages, each one trimmed in a different color paint. Flowering bushes were everywhere.

"The guest cottages are known by the color of the doors and trim," the older woman explained. "Yours is the Red Cottage, and when I said I'd have a tray sent *up,* I wasn't kidding," she said, laughing. "You're the last one up the hill."

"The view will be fabulous," Leda remarked, glancing behind her. *If I make it that far,* she thought wearily.

"Oh, quite. Normally I rent the Red Cottage, but it's so tiny that it's only comfortable, really, for one. And then, of course, the water pressure way up here . . . ah, here we are." They stopped at the door.

The twilight had deepened to near dark. Leda was not prepared for the magic of her view: a sweep of most of Admiralty Bay, the main harbor in Bequia. Dozens of yachts lay snugly at anchor, their riding lights twinkling and bobbing in the rigging. Green and red and yellow lamps from several restaurants and resorts picked out the shape of the shore for her, except for a long, dark stretch; that must be a beach. Across from where they stood, the businesslike fluorescence of the commercial dock lights bleared over a trading schooner and a small freighter. From a resort somewhere she heard the faint tinkle of a steel-drum band. And this fairyland was *home?* Tired as she was, she nearly danced on her doorstep. "I'm dreaming." She sighed.

"It's always the same the first day," Julie Simpson said thoughtfully. "You take me back to a night like this, oh, ten years ago or so. There were fewer harbor lights then, but the charm was—and is, my dear—still there. We're all little children down here."

They stepped inside the cottage, and Julie switched on a little red-shaded table lamp. More magic! Her cottage was actually a single room, with a louvered screen tucked in front of a small bed at one end, and a tiny refrigerator and hot plate at the other. The furniture was wicker and oak, and without pretension. The enchantment lay in the color scheme, a burst of deep reds and corals and oranges and rusts in a tumble of calicos and paisleys.

"I love it. I really do, Mrs. Simpson."

"You'll find that what we lack in variety down here, we make up in intensity. And call me Julie, for heaven's sake. I'm off to dinner. Thelma will bring your luggage up tomorrow morning, I'm sure. Sweet dreams, dear."

Leda pulled off her clothes in a heap and headed for the metal shower stall in the postage-stamp bathroom. The "shower" was more in the line of a strong trickle, and it wasn't terribly warm, but it did the job. Gingerly, Leda toweled herself dry. She had gotten perhaps a little burned. He *would* be right on the sunburn, too.

Clean but starving was how she felt. Wrapped in a terry-cloth towel, she was curled in a wicker chair, deep in meditation on the joys of pizza with mushrooms and pepperoni, when Thelma arrived with her real supper—curried lamb, rice with kidney beans, and warm bread. Ten minutes later, Leda was sipping her tea, convinced that no other mortal had ever dined as well. Ten minutes after that, she was stretched out luxuriously on

28

cool sheets, clad in a cream-colored slinky nightgown that Julie had sent up with Thelma.

The barest of breezes lifted the flaming calico curtain near the bed. Really, she thought sleepily, you didn't need curtains at all, way up here; they only blocked the breeze. . . .

In the moments before sleep, her head began spinning. Black barracuda swam round and round inside of it, and a black-bearded medieval knight pursued them from his flat-bottom boat, only now she was swimming among the barracuda, and the knight became a barracuda, and then she and the knight were in the boat, spinning round and round.

CHAPTER TWO

Leda awoke to the sound of sharp raps, but it took her several seconds to realize that it was early morning and that the knocking must be Thelma with her luggage. She staggered to the door, barely awake from her deep sleep, and opened it to find *him,* the knight, standing next to her three suitcases on the step.

She stared at him. "You're not Thelma," she said blankly.

"Very good," he answered dryly. "These are, however, your suitcases?" He stood there comfortably, taking in Leda's negligee with a cool and appraising look.

Fully awakened by the look, Leda jumped behind the door. "Yes. Well. Thank you. Ah . . . but you shouldn't have bothered. It's a hard climb up here." She realized the stupidity of her remark as her look fell to his well-developed thighs, flat stomach, and trim waist. He wore an unbuttoned flowered batik shirt over his khaki shorts; the soft, graceful material was in striking contrast to the muscled hardness of his midsection. He made no effort to help Leda end her limping monologue.

She gave him a brisk little smile. "I'd ask you in for a cup of coffee, but I haven't found the coffeepot yet. Perhaps another time."

"I'd be honored," he said with an ironic look.

Still he made no move to go. *Blast him!* She couldn't just close the door on his face. "The previous tenant was apparently a tea drinker," she plowed on stoically. "All bags and no grinds."

"Fine with me," he said. "Have you ever known an Englishman to refuse a spot of tea?" he asked blandly.

"Oh! But that's not what I . . . well, the tea is in bags, of course. And I've read that the British prefer their tea leaves loose." She had now reached complete incoherence. *You have the right to remain silent,* she insisted to herself. *Don't let him in, and don't open your mouth again.*

It worked. His eyes glittered through his sun-squint, and the amused look of tolerance disappeared. "I don't need a cup of tea enough to knock down a door for it, however," he said, scowling. Turning on his heel, he walked away.

Leda slammed the door on his retreating figure. Didn't the man ever sleep? Or did he just prowl the island, looking for devious new ways to embarrass her? Still, she'd won a small victory of sorts; she'd held him at bay. No doubt the soldiers inside the Alamo were, at some point, equally cheerful. She slipped on a pair of white cotton pants and a blue-gray softly tailored shirt. A silver bangle hung loosely on her slim wrist as she plaited her long hair into two braids and wrapped them into a frame around her oval face. She felt cool. She felt mature. She felt ready for Captain Hardy.

Now, on to the next phase: *Get down there fast, and show the other skippers that you're honest, intelligent, and reasonably modest. It's his word against yours.*

Out the door and down three steps, Leda turned suddenly to see her new home. In the morning's cool light the Red Cottage looked slightly less enchanting—the paint was a bit peely in spots—but it was gay and friendly. Tall, spiky tiger lilies knocked their heads on the windowsill next to her bed. Nearby bloomed huge kalanchoes; any resemblance to the petulant little houseplant she'd killed in her Newport apartment was strictly coincidental. Everything down here was bursting with life and energy. *And so am I,* she exulted. The next round would be hers.

On the veranda a dozen people were already breakfasting—including Julie—at a small table for two. Leda tapped on her watch crystal. Seven-thirty.

"Hi, Julie. Are all these people guests, or the night shift? I seem to be the last one up on Bequia."

"It's the only way to survive the heat down here. But the

31

system has its merits—we shut down for lunch from eleven to one or so in the afternoon," she promised with a smile.

Over breakfast Leda learned that all yacht charter services operated more or less in the same logical way. As in Newport, she would advertise the yachts that were available for charter, book the charter parties, see that the boats were ready to step aboard, and generally keep up the morale of the crews and guests who would be thrown together relentlessly for a week or two at a time.

"I have only one question," she concluded. "When I took the bus from Newport to Boston, a plane to Barbados, another plane to St. Vincent, a cab to the docks there, and a very wet speedboat ride to Bequia, was I *really* coming by the most direct route possible? Naturally I argued with the travel agent when he insisted I was." She smiled.

"Naturally you would; women love to argue," agreed a resonant voice behind her as a slow, totally irrational flush spread over her cheeks. "Anyway, that's the charm of Bequia," Hardy continued as he pulled up a chair. "None but the brave ever makes it to our little island to savor its slow pace, its unique people, its . . . deserted beaches."

He'd swung the chair around so that his forearms hung over the backrest; a thin cheroot angled rakishly from between even, white teeth. It was a jaunty performance. If you valued that sort of thing. She glared at him.

Julie glowed at him. "Natty! You've picked up Juanita in St. Vincent, then. How was dinner? Oh . . . Nathan Hardy, meet Leda Sayers, my new aide-de-camp." She turned to Leda. "Actually, he knows as much about you as I do. He looked over your resumé for me before I hired you."

Before she was hired! Who *was* this guy—the Godfather? "My goodness, Captain, you must be a force to be reckoned with around here." Leda managed to look suitably awestruck.

Hardy pulled an empty coffee cup toward him and knocked an ash into it. Blue eyes glittered under the visor of his black yachting cap. "When one woman hires another woman to run what is—by divine right—a man's world, you can *bet* there'll be

32

a man around keeping an eye on things." He took a long drag on his little cigar and blew a perfect smoke ring into the air.

Leda folded one arm over the other on the tiny table. "You're being facetious, of course. Julie? Isn't he?" she asked without taking her eyes from Nat's face.

"Oh, I don't think so, dear; Natty takes his boats very seriously." Obviously Julie wasn't the least bit offended by his chauvinism.

But Leda was. It was time to clear the air. "I take my boats very seriously, too, Captain. What makes you think I wouldn't?" she asked in a low, ominous voice.

"Miss Sayers . . . May I call you Leda?" he asked innocently. "Leda, you mean well, and you look perfectly competent, as far as women go. But don't y' see? It's a question of biology. A boat represents the opposite of the woman's nesting instinct. To work on or around boats you have to understand that they're symbols of restlessness, adventure, independence. But women . . . well, *women.* They like to settle in one place, put down roots, have a husband who's responsible for fixing everything. They hate being *on* boats, and most of 'em hate being *around* boats too."

She interrupted him. "I've never heard anything so stupid in all—"

"In all fairness, however," he interrupted her, "I *will* admit that women often work out very well down below in the galley. They're good at cooking, making cocktails, polishing the brass —and maybe one other thing." His grin was roguish.

This was a test. He couldn't possibly mean what he'd just said. He was just baiting her. She'd like to keelhaul him. She'd like to feed him to the sharks. She'd like to . . . to . . . Oh, that look in his eyes; that smile. It was how he'd looked when he kissed her in the brush yesterday. What . . . what was she thinking? Oh, right; that he was a male chauvinist.

"Captain, unless you've been marooned somewhere for the last ten years, you know as well as I do that women's attitudes have changed. They can be as restless, adventurous, and independent as you are. They're not afraid of flexing a little

33

muscle now and then, and—this may surprise you—they actually *enjoy* learning about something new."

Leda stood up, determined to leave while her emotions were still more or less under control. "Rest assured that I'll look after the *Swan*'s interests as if they were my own. Now if you'll excuse me . . ."

"Of course." He stood up with a surprisingly graceful movement. "I'll see you at eight," he said through a wisp of smoke.

"Oh now, *really* . . ." She could not believe that he intended to collect on yesterday's little piece of blackmail.

"A deal . . . is a deal."

"Deal?" Julie asked innocently.

Leda's smile was quick and bright. "Eight o'clock? Perfect. I can hardly wait." She positively beamed, and promptly dragged Julie offstage.

The rest of the day was at least a nominal success. Two of the charter skippers passed through the office, and Leda managed to act intelligent with one, modest with the other, according to plan. Late in the afternoon Julie wandered in, holding an overseas cable in her hand.

"I've just got a very nice wire from a couple in Illinois. They'd like to charter a sailboat of about fifty feet, with captain and crew, for their honeymoon. They want to come down next week—quite short notice, of course, but I gather the marriage is a whirlwind affair."

"Well, that shouldn't be a problem. It's still almost two weeks to Christmas and the high season; most of the yachts are free." Leda perused the calendar with a calculating eye, automatically dismissing the inappropriate boats. Only two seemed really suitable: Nat Hardy's *Swan* and a fifty-two-foot yawl, *Lorna Doone*.

Julie pointed out the two boats in the harbor. "Natty's *Swan* is the spotless new ketch just behind the big power boat. The *Lorna Doone* is farther out—the wooden boat with blue sail covers."

Leda, a great admirer of traditional wooden boats, was disappointed. "The *Lorna Doone* is a little tired-looking for a charter yacht, isn't she?"

Julie sighed. "I'm afraid so. They've only just arrived from New England. They had a terribly rough passage down here, and the *Lorna Doone* needs some sprucing up."

"I guess it's not much of a contest, then." Under "Hardy" Leda penciled in the name of the Illinois couple for the coming week. "I'll cable your newlyweds right now with the good news."

"You don't care to mention this to Natty first?" the older woman suggested.

"No, I don't think so. I see from the *Swan*'s sheet that it's scarcely booked at all this winter. One, two, only three charters all together. That's awful. I'm sure Captain Hardy will be pleased with the booking." Actually, she wasn't all *that* sure.

Again the older woman hesitated. "Natty is rather . . . particular, you know, about whom he takes."

Leda sighed. Nathan Hardy was going to be one of her difficult skippers. She'd dealt with them before. All ego, no business sense at all, and quite unjust to the actual owners of the yachts who were paying enormous upkeep—*and* the salaries of captain and crew.

"How can anyone possibly object to a honeymooning couple? I'm sure they'll be perfect clients. Naturally, I'll run the charter past Captain Hardy the next time I see him. Will that be all right with you?"

"Whatever you think is best, dear. The yacht part of Coco's has been sort of limping along ever since my husband died; I suppose it could use a little push right about now."

A great big *shove* is what the charter service needed, Leda decided at the end of the long hot day as she sat back at her desk, watching the sun drop low over the harbor, and reveling in the evening coolness. She was feeling not overly optimistic. Except for the Christmas and Easter periods, many weeks were still unbooked, especially for Hardy's *Swan*. The advertising copy she had seen so far was only so-so. And even the boats—

35

except for Hardy's *Swan* and one or two others—were not exactly in Bristol condition; nothing like the spit-and-polish look of her little Newport fleet.

Mañana. Everything down here was *mañana.* And in this heat, she could see why. An evening spent fencing with Nat Hardy would burn more calories than a good workout in a gym: parry and thrust, feint and lunge. Too much work. *How about dinner* mañana *instead of tonight, Captain Hardy?* She cast a look, not for the first time, at the *Swan,* anchored out of reach in the middle of the harbor. Darn. She couldn't even telephone her regrets.

The cure for terminal weariness turned out to be one trickly shower and a transfusion of strong tea. Gone was the listlessness; in Leda's veins instead surged a maddening expectancy. Probably it's the caffeine, she told herself as she traced a hint of eye shadow across her lids and lightly drew a stick of lip gloss over her full, sensuous mouth.

One nice thing about the Caribbean, she decided gratefully, was the ease with which one dressed. The concept of panty hose did not exist down here. Dresses were designed to be cool, to be comfortable, and to be worn without bras, which was how Leda wore the softly patterned mauve sundress that she'd bought on a frantic lunch-hour search. Cut well down in the back, the simple design complemented the soft, full curves of Leda's tall, rounded figure, and the color flattered the hint of sunburn that lingered on her cheeks and nose. A necklace of dark coral beads echoed the tiny flowers in the dress pattern.

She tossed off an automatic smile at the mirror to check her makeup. Leda-on-the-wall gave Leda-in-the-flesh a sudden, wry look. *Nice outfit. Any particular reason why we're dressing to kill tonight?*

No reason, no reason, the real Leda hummed.

Two minutes to eight. The steady beat of her heart grew mysteriously into a loud thumping as she brushed the last remaining dampness from her hair. *Why are you behaving like an imbecile?* she demanded. Instantly her analytical mind flashed three possible reasons for a rapid heartbeat: fear, sex, or anger. Probably, she told herself against all the evidence, it was anger. She brushed her hair more briskly. The hairbrush caught in the strand of her necklace, breaking it, and a little red army of coral beads skittered across the varnished floor in all directions.

"Nuts. *Nuts!*" she nearly shouted with vexation.

The door swung open. Leda looked up from her position on the floor to see Nat Hardy, an enormous, illogical bunch of bright flowers in his arms, standing on the threshold. He looked quizzical and as close to shy as he probably ever got. The expression was altogether at odds with the strong, commanding features of the man.

All Leda's pent-up feelings flew off on the wings of a merry laugh. "Whatever it is you're 'saying with flowers,' I'm impressed."

She sat back on the floor. "I've just broken my coral necklace; beads are *every*where. You know," she said wistfully, "just *once* I'd like to meet you when I was feeling poised, and fully dressed, and preferably standing on my own two feet."

"You wouldn't say that if you knew how fetching you look just now," he said with a pensive smile.

A little embarrassed by Nat's look, Leda rose to take the flowers from him, but he stopped her. "Go on with the hunt; I'll put these in water."

A milk pitcher sat on a shelf too high for Leda ever to reach. He pulled it down, plopped the flowers into it, and ran the tap. "Actually, down here it's considered wicked, bad form to show up at your girl's house without a bouquet."

Leda's immediate impulse was to challenge his offhand reference to her as his "girl," but she stifled it, without being certain why.

"Two of the little devils are up against the wall, under the sofa. Your arm's longer than mine, Nat; would you mind?"

"For you, anything." He reached under, and Leda, still on her knees, took advantage of his distraction to indulge in a long, unguarded scrutiny. His bearded cheek lay next to the floor; with a painful jolt Leda realized that he would have just that

37

expression as he lay on a pillow. The back of his tanned neck, next to the pale blue linen of his shirt, was deep brown. His black hair was thick and neatly combed, and Leda beat back an urge to rumple it up for him.

Nat scooped up the beads, and sitting back on his calves, extended his fist to Leda to give them to her. But into her open palm he dropped, instead, an Eastern Caribbean penny.

"A penny? Where'd you get that?"

"Under the couch."

"What's it for?"

"Your thoughts. That was quite an appraising look I got just now."

Caught red-handed in the cookie jar. "How did you know?"

"Felt the back of my neck prickle. You have that effect on me, you know," he said equably.

"Well, if you must know, I was wondering why you weren't in movies."

Nat didn't exactly blush; his tan was too concealing to allow other than a slightly deeper shading to cross his face. But she knew she had knocked him off balance for once, and the realization gave her a quirky little rush of, well, *power*.

"That's a silly line of talk," he said gruffly.

"Sorry," she returned with ironic politeness. "I promise not to look at you again."

"Don't be impertinent, child," Nat said more mildly. "Here's your coral beads. Quite nice ones too, I might add. That deep shade is rare nowadays."

"I got them in Bermuda a couple of years ago. I also got a case of island fever there. Of course, Bermuda is nothing like Bequia, I see now. In Bermuda it's so much cooler—and more sophisticated."

"You have something against heat and simplicity?" he asked, amused.

"They take getting used to," she confessed as they moved toward the door.

"Wait. That dress needs a jewel." Carefully he broke off a red hibiscus from the bouquet and placed it in the deep vee of her

38

bodice; his touch was light as silk. Leda was torn between wonder that hands so strong could be so sure, and a devastating realization that Nat Hardy could not touch her without leaving a trail of crackling awareness of where he had been.

"It suits you," he said simply.

The sigh that escaped Leda seemed to come from lips other than her own. Her voice was barely a whisper. "It . . . won't . . . stay in place, of course." The exotic red blossom accentuated the uneven rise and fall of her breast as she drew breath.

Nat's feather touch traced the outline of her hair, and Leda felt her nerve endings tingle with pleasurable response. "Your hair is so silky," he said thoughtfully. "Do you think the hibiscus would slip away if we tucked it behind your ear?" His hand trailed a path from the ends of her hair, across the top of her dress to the flaming blossom, and there it lingered. "Should we try?" he murmured, as though the issue were of great importance.

"We . . . could try," she acquiesced helplessly.

With infinite tenderness he lifted the flower from between Leda's breasts and tucked it in her hair. His black brows drew together in concentration. "It won't . . . well, it might . . . no, it won't . . . stay. Will it?" he asked hopefully.

"Probably not," she answered with a soft, sweet smile. *The most practical thing,* she wanted to tell him, *would be for you to hold it there for the rest of the evening.*

"I'll braid it through a strand of your hair, then. If it takes every knot I know, you'll wear this flower."

His broad shoulders loomed over her, an obstacle around which she must navigate carefully if she were ever to breathe normally again. *Eyes up, steady as she goes, there.* But her lids fluttered, then lowered, to hide the aroused wonder her eyes surely would have betrayed.

His head bent over hers. "Leda, pretty island belle . . ." His lips touched hers with a butterfly's caress. Perhaps she imagined the touch. And then they returned, to brush her mouth again, and then again, lingering longer on each visit, tasting and sampling each little section of her lips as if it were an entirely new treat to be savored. His tongue teased the corner of her mouth, then rolled gently over her lower lip before it explored more deeply. The oddly exciting tickle of his mustache and the faint taste of a cheroot combined to make his kisses strange, urgent, somehow grown-up—two thousand light years away from Jeffrey's downy blond chin and breath fresheners.

"Nat . . . Nat . . ." she whispered. With a will all their own, her arms reached up around his neck. Like Alice, she was falling irreversibly into a Wonderland of terror and delight. Had she eaten Alice's little currant cake as well? Because she seemed to be growing, bursting from within—it was Nat, rubbing her swelling nipples with his hands to an unbearable pitch through the soft fabric of her dress.

She had to get back; this was too new, too frightening, too much of a free-fall for a girl whose two feet were used to being planted firmly on the ground. She pulled away, gasping for breath. "Where am I?" she panted.

"Seventh planet out and still orbiting," he murmured. "No need to return just yet; there's another shuttle in an hour."

"Let's take this one, Nat, please," she whispered. "I need to decompress."

"Actually, I'm not *all* that hungry," he said with a hopeful grin.

Still shaky with desire, Leda managed with a violent effort to turn an emotional somersault. "No siree, you dealt me a dinner, and a dinner I get." Anything to get them out of the cottage and into the cool, rational night.

He ushered her out of the cottage into the pitch-black. "Moon's not up yet. Good lord, I can't see a thing. This is outrageous. Why hasn't Julie had a lamp installed at the top of the step path?" His hand reached out around Leda's shoulder to detain her. "We'll stand still for a moment until our eyes adjust; or else one of us will break an ankle."

Leda stood next to him quietly, drinking in the sweet, aromatic night. Nat slipped one arm around her and gently nipped the lobe of her beflowered ear.

40

"What *is* it about you, dammit; I could devour you whole," he murmured in a husky voice.

"Bones and all, I'll bet," she agreed briskly, fighting an impulse to meet his lips again. The air was warm and sultry and not in the least cool or rational. "We're becoming later and later for dinner, don't you think? I can see just fine now. Let me lead you," she offered.

"No, no, I can see, too, now. *I'll* lead," he said almost petulantly as he took her hand and struck out down the path.

Leda smiled in the blackness behind him. He was used to being the dominant force, that was clear. And it wasn't hard to see why. He was so charged with sexuality that no woman who still had two or more of her five senses could resist him. Maybe it was the beard. Beards gave men a sense of mystery and remoteness. Beards also hid double chins or weak lower jaws, of course; but that would not be the case with this man. She remembered that Jeffrey had tried a beard once; and it was true, the beard did hide a sort of . . . irresoluteness in Jeffrey's face. How odd that she had never considered Jeffrey in that light before.

The restaurant was in Port Elizabeth, the tiny main town in Bequia, and the distance they walked equaled no more than three or four city blocks. Leda laughed as she recalled being hopelessly lost earlier.

Nat joined in. "Port Elizabeth didn't even have a *name* until 1937. You were expecting exit ramps and cloverleafs perhaps?"

"Certainly not; merely something in an occasional paved surface. But I'm not complaining. Bequia is just what I had in mind: remote, interesting, and lively."

"Precisely what your Yankee ancestors thought a hundred years ago when they jumped ship, swam ashore, mingled, and married." From across the table he caught, then held, her look. "What've you enjoyed the most, so far?"

"The little goats that run around everywhere," she answered promptly. "They're adorable."

"Shhh." He lowered his voice. "That's pronounced 'lamb' around here," he whispered confidentially.

A lump formed in her throat. "You mean, as in 'curried'?"

"Mmm-hmmn." He leaned back in his chair, stroking his mustache and looking poetically demonic in the red light of the candle globe.

The waitress arrived, and with Nat's assurance Leda allowed herself to be guided through a culinary maze beginning with callaloo soup, made with crab and spinachlike leaves of callaloo, and ending with custard-covered mango pie. "Unless you'd prefer the curried lamb?" he inquired politely.

"I've had some recently, thanks." She smiled gamely.

When they were alone again, she gave him a worried little smile. "Nat, one thing that's still bothering me . . ."

"Yes?"

"It's that stupid car; it really would not start."

"Of course it wouldn't."

"How will I *ever* convince you!" she cried in exasperation.

"You silly twit. The ignition wire had come loose; does it all the time. I just reconnected it when you were groping in your handbag."

A dull flush slowly overspread her cheeks. Her heartbeat took off and yes, she decided clinically, the reason definitely was anger. "What a rotten trick! You left me thinking that I'd made a jerk of myself, and thinking you'd have a great story to—"

"—malign your character with, up and down the length, such as it is, of Bequia? Is that what you take me for? Leda," he complained gently, "that was a bit of fun between you and me. I'm sorry if you took it too seriously."

He made a movement toward her face with his hand, and Leda jumped back in her chair. "If you think you can just pinch my cheek and say, 'Smile, you're so much cuter then,' well, you're wrong."

He looked startled. "No, I was going to . . . I don't know, stroke your cheek, I think. You looked so lovely in the candlelight. It's hard not to touch you, Leda."

Her fury melted like hot wax under the flame of his voice. Where was righteous anger when you needed it?

The sweet potato bread arrived, and Nat buttered a huge slab for each of them. "Tell me about your family. I'll bet your childhood was outrageously normal," he prompted her.

"Two parents, one of each sex and married happily—oddly—to one another. One sister, very dear. And a brother, twelve years old and true to type. You're right; it *is* outrageous. How about you?"

"An only child," he said briefly, and abruptly changed the subject. "So what do you know about boats?"

She shrugged. "A fair amount. I grew up on the coast of Maine."

"Any boats in the family?"

"Mostly knockabouts and dinghies, unless you count my second cousin's lobster boat. But all I know about lobstering, you could fit in one claw."

"Where *did* you learn about big yachts, in that case?"

Persistent, wasn't he? "I . . . ah . . . went out with someone who owned a sailboat."

"Oh? What kind?" Nat took a large bite of his bread.

"Just a garden-variety forty-foot sloop. It had been in the family, and when his father died, he chose to keep it for a couple of years."

"An heir, is he? How interesting. What does he do for a living, our young man?"

"Jeffrey," she interrupted.

"Pardon?"

"Jeffrey. His name is Jeffrey. He's *not* 'our young man.' You make it sound as though he's our son. Let me try some of your flying fish pie," she demanded, hoping to get him off the subject of Jeffrey.

"Jeffrey, then. This Jeffrey . . . you were fond of him?"

"Yes." She sighed. Jeffrey was becoming a third guest at the table.

"*How* fond?"

"Fond enough to become engaged, and if you *don't* mind, I'd rather not talk about it. Are you going to eat the rest of that?" she asked, pointing to the last slice of uneaten bread.

"You have the appetite of a young warrior, Leda," Nat observed with genuine surprise. "How do you burn it all off?"

"I worry a lot. Look, Nat, maybe we'd better just get Jeffrey over with. He's ruining my dinner."

"He's ruining *mine.*"

She gave him a quizzical look. Why all this interest in her love life? And why was she about to tell Nat what she had avoided telling any other living soul? "I thought Jeffrey and I were engaged—or at least, that we had an understanding. We were together a lot of the time. We talked about the future, went off to Nantucket for the weekend, did all the things that serious couples do. It's true we never actually set a date; the subject never came up, somehow. Anyway"—she took a long, deep breath and exhaled slowly—"anyway I found him in bed with a woman. And that was that. Finished." There. It was out. And it didn't hurt as much as she'd always assumed it would.

"Leda, anyone can have a moment of weakness," he argued softly.

Well, what had she expected? "I suppose your reaction is typical—for a man. Will it help my case if I told you that in the discussion that followed, I found out that it wasn't the first time? Jeffrey was a member of half a dozen different clubs and committees in Newport. On the Save the Ships Committee the vice-chairperson happened to be a gorgeous blond. A sparkling brunette worked at the reception desk of the racquetball club where Jeffrey played. And the artist who designed the posters for his 'Conservatives for a Better Newport'?—five feet eight inches of auburn dynamite. Do you need any more exhibits? Or may the prosecution rest?" she asked wearily

"Leda, why are you doing this to yourself?" He had been twisting the stem of his wineglass round and round, and Leda had been focusing intently on the black curly hairs on the back of his hand as she blurted out her secret. When he looked up at her, his brows were angled toward one another in a look of uncharacteristic sympathy. Nat Hardy, the rakish Nat Hardy, sympathetic? *Get serious, girl.*

"Why *am* I telling you this?" She tried to laugh it off. "I suppose, to prove to myself that it doesn't matter. He was just being typical. It was painful at the time, I won't deny it—lots of second-guessing and hand-wringing."

"You had no idea what was going on?" he asked quietly.

"No, why should I? I trusted him; it never occurred to me *not* to. Since then I've come to regard 'trust' as a phase you pass through, like measles and mumps and your first crush."

"You're absolutely right," he agreed surprisingly.

"Well *that's* a switch," she admitted. "Aren't you supposed to tell me to *keep on* trusting people?"

"Wrong. If you're going to survive as a resident of Paradise, you'd better learn to keep your guard up. People wander down to the islands looking for pleasure. As a rule they find it." The meal had wound down to coffee and liqueur, and Nat had lit the inevitable cheroot. "Soulful unions and long-term commitments are out of place here."

"You're telling me that I've just moved from the seaport of temptations to the island of the one-night stand? Wonderful," she said dryly. She swirled and warmed a snifter of cognac in the palm of her hand. "Why did you ask me to dinner, really?" she asked suddenly.

"Not because you're a pretty face," he answered without hesitation. "Those are taken for granted down here."

That, Leda had already discovered. Every other woman in the restaurant seemed far more beautiful than she.

"It's partly to make up for our rocky start yesterday. I want us to work easily together," he continued methodically.

Very good. So did she. Perhaps he was more professional than she'd guessed.

"But it's mostly because you're a . . . puzzle."

"Puzzle?"

"Yes. You simply don't fit the usual picture of a pretty, twenty-six-year-old arrival to the Caribbean. Most women would move their three little suitcases promptly aboard the first yacht that offered to take 'em in—as 'crew.' They'd be down here for a *very* good time, and if now and then they did some

45

work to earn their keep, well, the skipper counts himself lucky. Loyalties mean nothing. Female crews jump ship all the time."

"You have a pretty shabby view of women, I think," Leda answered, with a sadness that surprised her.

"That depends on how you look at it. Very few people down here are what you New Englanders"—he emphasized "New Englanders" as though they were a strange Martian race—"would consider goal-oriented. The idea, down here, is to do a reasonable amount of work and have a damn good time doing it. Life is fleeting, but the Caribbean manages to slow it down and stretch it out a bit."

He pulled out Leda's chair for her. "Now *you* are an empire builder, and a workaholic to boot. I saw that in your resumé. There's even a rumor going around that you only take half an hour for lunch!"

She laughed. *"That* will change. It's physically impossible to push through that noon wall of heat. I think I'd be more efficient if I took a two-hour lunch like everyone else."

They ambled through the darkened main street, pausing before a neatly painted Anglican church which was fronted by a tiny yard filled with flowering plants and a very large bronze bell.

"A church bell in the front yard!" Leda folded her arms over the fence and swayed softly to a melody of delight that insisted on playing itself over and over in her head. "It's almost too charming to believe; it doesn't still work, by any chance?"

"You bet your bell ringer it still works; rings regularly, in the dead of night." He was standing close to her, one arm resting on the fence. With an idle, gentle movement he settled the hibiscus back into her hair.

It started Leda's heart galloping off like a runaway pony. "Why should the bell ring at strange hours?" she asked weakly, her senses on full-scale alert for further symptoms of cardiac arrest. "Is the churchyard haunted?"

"Regularly, my little seahorse—by yachties *and* Bequians. The nocturnal bell ringer generally is three sheets to the wind and jolly well eager to let the rest of us know it."

46

Leda was shocked. "You mean, *drunks* come into the church-yard and ring the church bell?"

"One hundred and nineteen times on a good—excuse me, a bad—night recently. Not all of them are drunk, though. First-time fathers and newly engaged bucks have been known to, well, succumb, out of sheer happiness."

"How awful! What does the minister say?"

"Depends if he catches you or not," Nat answered cheerfully. "Let's go back along the beach."

"I thought you'd never ask," she said, pleased.

"You really are an ocean sprite, aren't you? Are you quite certain there are no Ahabs or Hornblowers in your family tree?"

"Absolutely. Any in yours?"

To her surprise, his answer was straightforward and even expansive. "I was born on a boat, actually. My parents were on an eight-year circumnavigation when I made an appearance during the third year, in Singapore. I was five when they arrived back in England, and apparently I put up such a fuss about not being able to play rugby and cricket like the rest of my country-men that they moved back ashore for my sake. What they should have done is lock me up in the fo'c'sle until I reached the age of reason and could value the experience."

"You remember none of your trip around the world, then?" She was disappointed.

"Precious little. I remember Pitcairn Island in the Pacific, mostly because the descendants of the original *Bounty* muti-neers still speak English there, and I could communicate with them. The rest is a bit of a blur."

The two paused on the hard, damp sand and stared out at the yachts in the harbor. A brilliant moon cast a bright fluorescence over the scene, then tucked behind a cloud and cast them into blackness. Suddenly subdued, Leda groped for something com-forting to say.

"Don't you think it was important for you to live ashore and learn how to, well, get along with others?"

Nat turned and gripped her by her shoulders as he searched

47

her face in his determination to make her understand. "Look, Leda, on my parents' boat I learned about family love and commitment. I learned independence, resourcefulness, the humility that comes from getting through a storm at sea in one piece. Ashore . . . ashore I learned to be competitive, businesslike, and ruthless. Is that what you mean by 'getting along'?"

"Of course not, Nat, I . . ." Leda winced as he continued to hold her tightly.

Immediately he released his hold. "I'm sorry, that was incredibly stupid of me. Let me try this again. They say 'you only go around once,' right? Five years ago, when I was twenty-nine, I tried to go 'around,' literally, a second time. I put my business in the hands of a crack management outfit, bought a boat, and set off from England, happy as a clam at high tide."

"It sounds like you were living a very popular dream," Leda said softly.

"Hardly. Before we were a hundred miles out, my wife was so seasick that she threatened to jump overboard if I didn't head back to England. Everyone gets sick the first day or two, of course—I wasn't feeling too grand myself—but she panicked."

My wife. The shock wave that swept over Leda at that instant measured 6.5 on the Richter scale.

"So we turned around," he continued, without looking at Leda, as though he were still ashamed. "We moved everything off the boat, sold it, and soon after went our separate ways. It was like watching a movie being run in reverse."

Still a bit stunned, Leda said, "I don't know what to say." Her mind was working on another track altogether. "Separate ways." What did *that* mean? Separation? Divorce? Open marriage? "Separate ways" was very imprecise. In an exquisite agony, Leda trailed alongside the tall captain. Her whole body ached with awareness of him, but he seemed in another world, totally oblivious of her.

"It was devastating," he muttered.

"Your . . . going separate ways?" she whispered.

He looked at her sharply. "Of course not. I meant, having to face the world after loftily announcing plans to sail *around* it. We were even an 'item' in the *London Times*. Twice. Setting out, and then returning," he said bitterly.

"Did your wife have any sailing experience at all?"

"Mostly weekend yachting in the Mediterranean. Anne-Marie was a wonderful fraud; the type who believed all the stories she made up about herself. It would've been churlish not to believe along with her."

"Perhaps she just didn't have enough time to adapt." Leda was sounding more and more like a counsel for the defense.

"She had all the time she's going to get, I'm afraid," he said tersely. "After the mis— We were divorced a few months later. And from all that," he continued in the same weary voice, "I have learned two lessons: Don't get involved, and *never* take a woman to sea."

"Oh, now, that isn't fair," she protested earnestly. "Just because your wife didn't work out doesn't mean every woman is incompetent at sea."

"They don't have the strength, and they don't have the stomachs," he said abruptly.

"Yes they *do!*"

"No—they don't. Here," he said, pausing under the low branches of a tree. "This'll do for a test. Grab this branch and chin yourself on it."

"Certainly," she said, angered and feeling very strong. She reached up; it was too high. She made a jump at it; still too high.

He sighed. "I'll lift you up." His hands circled her waist and raised her effortlessly to the branch. "Got it?"

She took a deep breath. "Yes. Let go."

"Ho-kay, you're on your own."

With his support withdrawn, her weight seemed suddenly enormous. Still, whether it was the wine, or his seasick wife, or his arrogance, or Leda's fierce desire to prove herself—she raised herself to the branch, inch by fraction of an inch, her temples pounding with the effort, and touched it lightly with

49

her chin, then dropped like a stone into his outstretched arms. "There!"

He caught her easily and lowered her slowly to the ground. She was aware of every square inch of her uncovered back as she stood cradled against his chest. Someone inside of her counted one, two, three buttons on his linen shirt. His hands slid from the sides of her waist to her belly, and his flat palms, fingers spread, moved slowly up and down the vee formed by her thighs and torso.

The soft panting of her recent exertion became deeper and more urgent as she stood in the darkness, unconsciously pressing her weight back into him. He nuzzled the nape of her neck through her thick golden hair. "So I was wrong," he murmured. "You do have the strength." His hands slid lightly up and down the fabric of her dress, from her thighs, across her midriff, to just below her breasts.

Her last deep breath had become almost a moan as Leda whispered, "Nat . . . hold me." He knew, without asking, what her simple request meant, and his hands slid over her breasts, circling them lightly in smaller and smaller movements until his touch was entirely on her swelling, throbbing nipples.

Was she even wearing a dress? In her dazed, aching state she thought not. She shuddered under wave after wave of novel, surging desire. It was all so . . . new. "Nat," she moaned softly. "Please . . . more."

"Ah, Leda . . . more . . . is what there is. More . . ." He turned her toward him, trailing his lips in a scorching line along the curve of her shoulder. "And more . . ." He slipped her dress straps over her shoulders and slid the thin fabric down below her elbows, lowering his mouth to the fullness of her rising, falling breasts. "Oh, darlin', and still more," he murmured as he knelt before her, flicking his tongue lightly over her nipple.

Her arms hung down by her sides, and her hands rested on the solid forearms that held her bottom firmly toward his chest. Her breath now came in long, ragged sighs, and she promised herself that when he drew his mouth away from her breast, she

50

would stop it all. But then he began to kiss her other nipple, and she knew that she could not stop until . . . until after that.

From a few feet away she heard the soft lapping of the ocean, and in her hazy arousal she thought it was the sound of the waves of desire that were flooding over her.

I'll drown, I really will drown, if I stay here, she thought.

"Leda," he rasped in a shaken, low voice, "let me make love to you."

"And if I . . . drown?" she asked, faintly puzzled and almost sleepy with passion.

"We'll go down together," he murmured, gently pulling the straps of her dress up and walking alongside, one arm wrapped around her slim back to support her.

The short walk back steadied her wobbly legs, and the climb up the hill steadied her equally wobbly nerves. By the time they had reached her door she was capable of stringing real sentences, with subjects and verbs, back to back.

Her little set speech, rehearsed along the way, was straightforward enough when she ran through it in her mind: *Nat, this is too much, too soon. It's also too electric, too often. Jeffrey was nothing like this, and I'm scared emotionally and uneasy professionally. And besides that, I don't, I can't, trust you.*

But with her bare back to her door, what she really said was, "Nat, I don't feel very well."

The eyebrow and the tiny scar below it raised up quizzically. "Oh? Nothing to do with dinner, I hope."

"Not at all. It's just that . . ." Her look was wistful and longing, but the little crease in her forehead told her story all too plainly.

His smile was rueful. "It's okay," he said gently. "Down here there's always *mañana,* fair one."

"Good night, Nat," she whispered, illogically sorry.

"Good night . . . may I kiss you good night?" His voice was suddenly irresistibly tender. Leda closed her eyes.

He was as good as his word and kissed Leda, once. She might just as well have been struck by lightning, once. Once was all it took for her initial reluctance to melt away into a gasping surge of desire. His hands traced the curve of her back and the flare of her hips from her waist. One arm encircled her, drawing her up close to his massive, hard chest; the other flattened her lower torso against his own; and his sudden, urgent need penetrated the swirl of her consciousness.

It was a brief, breathless, rocketing ride into ecstasy. When it was over, Nat let her back to earth gently with tender kisses along the nape of her neck. She clung to him, as much to prolong the hot sweetness of his touch as to steady her wavering frame.

He pulled back and looked at her closely, still supporting her. "Hey . . . are you all right, Leda?"

Slowly her eyes refocused on his concerned face. "Of course, I'm all right. Why wouldn't I be? Good night, Nat."

He dropped his mouth to hers in a light farewell, turned down the step path, and was swallowed by the night.

In her cottage, Leda closed the door behind her and leaned back on it, breathing quickly or forgetting to breathe, she was not sure which. "I'm not all right," she said aloud. "I'm in big trouble."

CHAPTER THREE

It must have been the wine. Leda popped two aspirins and reminded herself, again, that alcohol was not for her. Last night eight ounces of chablis had worked some fierce black magic in her soul. Before dinner Nat Hardy had seemed . . . interesting. After dinner, she'd have taken a number and waited in line for him. It had to be the wine.

She pulled a yellow blouse over her head and wrapped a flowered skirt around her waist, feeling remarkably like a violin after a premiere performance by a virtuoso. She'd been entirely in Nat's hands, and he'd made her rise or fall, glide or soar, at will. Who would have guessed that she was capable of such song? Certainly not Jeffrey, she decided ruefully. She'd flown two thousand miles to be free of one man's lukewarm hold, only to end up tyrannized by this . . . this petty dictator in a ten-square-mile kingdom. Eat this. Eat that. Who's Jeffrey? Keep your guard up. He knew her inside and out. He'd even got her to say . . . What *hadn't* he got her to say!

But *she* didn't even know if Nat Hardy had remarried. He might be a bigamist! Who would know, with his life-style? He could have a wife in Antigua, another one in Curaçao, one on every other island in the Caribbean, for that matter. Not that it really mattered. He was so patently unsuitable for . . . whoever. He was too handsome, too good at lovemaking, too independent, too knowledgeable.

In the middle of brushing her teeth she paused. *Very good, Ms. Sayers. You've just tried to tell yourself that you'd prefer someone homely, clumsy, helpless, and stupid. Do get a grip on yourself, will you?*

53

The sorrowful truth was that Leda Sayers had once again failed, in a most spectacular way, to show that she could "keep her guard up." Out of the arms of one playboy, and into the arms of another. And yet, unlike Jeffrey, Nat had made *his* intentions perfectly clear. So why resent him for it? The obvious answer was to distance herself from him, mentally plaster a HIGH VOLTAGE—KEEP AWAY sign on his chest. And never, of course, wear a backless dress again.

She stepped outside her tiny cabin and was once again bowled over by the sunshine glory of the Caribbean morning. Automatically she scanned the harbor for new yacht arrivals and departures. The *Swan* was gone.

At breakneck speed Leda ran down the steps to her office. Nat had a charter to pick up Sunday. But he didn't know he had a charter Sunday. The timing had never seemed quite right last night, and Leda had convinced herself that the business could be left to daytime hours. Coward! Fool! She had only herself to blame. Why hadn't he said he was leaving? Secretive, horrible man!

Breathless, she accosted Julie Simpson in the lobby. "The *Swan* isn't in the harbor; where has Nat gone?"

"Now that's hard to say," Julie considered calmly. "He may have sailed to Union Island. Or to Mustique for a few days." Then she brightened. "Probably he sailed to St. Vincent to stock up on groceries for that charter."

"How could he?" Leda wailed. "He doesn't even *know* about it."

Julie's look of surprise put Leda on the defensive. "I planned to tell him this morning," she answered quickly. "That was *so* dumb."

"Oh, well, things will work out. They always do," Julie said pleasantly.

Leda stared at her in wide-eyed apoplexy. How did the woman do it? Drugs? Hypnosis? Absolutely nothing seemed to faze her.

Julie's smile was wonderfully free of condescension. "I know you think I'm underreacting, dear; but there's just no reason to get alarmed yet."

"You're absolutely right, Julie," Leda decided grimly. "I'll just sit tight for a while."

And tight she sat, right through lunch and part of the afternoon, scanning the harbor every three or four minutes. In theory, she was rewriting ad copy for their American market. In practice, she was just this side of a nervous breakdown.

And then she spied the unmistakably lofty mast of the *Swan* on the horizon. Nat was bearing down on Admiralty Bay under full sail, an image of grace and speed.

"It's Nat; he's back!" Her heart did a high bounce of relief and unrelated, infuriating joy.

"My goodness, Leda, you're taking this far too seriously," Julie admonished. "We would have managed somehow without him."

"We *certainly* would have," she agreed briskly. She was thinking, as she said that, that the *Swan* was the most beautiful little ship.

"Do you dislike Natty?" Julie asked curiously.

"Dislike? Oh, hardly that. I don't know enough about him. Except, of course, that he seems to despise his ex-wife more than the average divorced man." Leda was fishing for more on Nat, and she knew it. She wasn't disappointed; the older woman rose to the bait.

"Then you've heard about their trip; an extremely awkward business. Friends of mine in London knew them both. The wife, Anne-Marie, was apparently a soaring star in London society—terribly rich, of course, and simply glittering with good looks. Bright, gay, and, well, the kindest word for it is *adventurous*. Poor Natty. He mistook what she called adventure for his own ideas on the subject. Her idea of adventure was to prowl London after hours looking for excitement," Julie said with a look of distaste.

She looked down at the weekly menu she'd been planning. "What do you think, dear? Will there be an uprising if I substitute conch for lobster in the salad tomorrow night?" Then without waiting for an answer she made a notation and returned to her rambling monologue. "Anyway, I can't say I blame Anne-Marie. Who could bear being *out* there, on the ocean, without a telephone or a doctor or newspapers or television or even street-lights, for heaven's sake."

Leda laughed. "This, from the one who fled the streetlights of London over ten years ago for the primitive joys of Bequia?"

"My dear, I *flew* over the Atlantic; I didn't try to *float* over it in a little box which could be sunk by some beastly whale at any given moment. *That* is primitive."

"Oh, I don't know," Leda mused as she watched the *Swan* spread its wings across the surface of the water. "I find it a very . . . very appealing notion."

Julie watched her curiously. "Who told you about Anne-Marie, incidentally?"

"He did."

"*Did* he now?" she asked thoughtfully.

The two women watched the boat bear down on their end of the harbor. Closer and closer it tacked, adeptly maneuvering under sail between the crowded yachts at anchor. A flotilla of tiny Bequia sloops, twelve feet overall and painted rainbow colors, butterflied in and out around the white-winged *Swan*. Young Bequians, their dark faces contrasting with the faded linen sails of their little boats, screamed with laughter. The charm of the scene completely dispelled the somber mood Julie's story had created, and Leda found herself, like Nat, determined to put Anne-Marie behind her.

The office was only a stone's throw from the beach, and the *Swan* was heading for them like a thoroughbred to the finish line. "My God, he's going to run aground!" Leda cried.

"Oh, Natty's just showing off," Julie answered mildly. "He knows this harbor like the back of his hand."

Within yards of the beach, Nat rounded up smartly, dropped an anchor, and doused the huge jib. The mainsail was dropped next. The maneuver was performed confidently, expertly, and with an obvious awareness of its spectacular effect. Exhibitionist.

56

With the sails furled out of the way, Leda for the first time registered that Nat was not alone. Helping him put the *Swan* in order was a lithe, tawny-skinned woman wearing a pair of drawstring white shorts and an almost negligible bikini top. Her face was protected from the ravages of the sun by a red visor, and her long, shining black hair was loose and trailing in the strong breeze.

"Julie," Leda began in a barely even tone, "do you know who the woman is, helping Nat furl the sails?"

Julie looked up from her work and peered over at the *Swan*. "Certainly. That's Juanita. You haven't met her yet?"

"No-o," Leda admitted, remembering that Nat had picked her up the night Leda arrived. She didn't look like a sister, somehow. Probably she was one of his island wives.

"Juanita is his crew, of course," Julie answered. "She's been away on holiday, visiting relatives in Rio."

"She's Brazilian?"

"Her mother is. Her father is American, and I must say, the combination produced an absolutely stunning daughter. Wait until you do meet her."

I can wait, Leda thought wearily. So Nat Hardy had a female crew aboard his boat. Their relationship was probably reasonably exclusive; just an occasional dinner—or kiss—or whatever it took, with someone else, to relieve the boredom of a steady diet of one person in confined quarters. *He can't have steak every day; I bring a little macaroni and cheese into his life.*

From miles away Julie's voice came to her. "Leda, I'll be going over the menu in the kitchen if you need me."

"Mmm? Oh, okay." It was time to collect what was left of her wits and advise Nat about the charter. How she'd manage it, she had no idea. Borrow a dinghy and row out to tell him? Send a note in a bottle? Smoke signals? Drumbeats?

"Hello, love. You called?"

"Ah?" She jumped no more than an inch. He stood in the doorway, one shoulder leaning against the frame, a cheroot clamped between his teeth—every woman's notion of the consummate rake.

"*Must* you always strike a pose?" she asked, irritated by her edginess. "And *who* said I wanted to see *you?*"

He laughed. "Just about every kid on Bequia, as a matter of fact."

"Oh. Well, I may have mentioned something to one or two of them," she replied coolly.

Unfolding his lanky frame from the door frame, he crossed the room in three strides, bent over, and kissed Leda lightly on the nose. "Incidentally, guess what day this is," he said softly.

She wanted to scream, *The day before the day before your charter, you dope!* But she couldn't say that. Or anything else. She seemed to have lost, for a variety of reasons, her faculty of speech. "Uh . . . what? Day?"

"It's *mañana,* and *mañana,* as the song says, is good enough for me." His voice radiated warmth and high hope at her. "Where shall we dine tonight?"

"You can dine at the Waldorf for all I care," she said, locating her tongue. "That is not why I wanted to see you."

"Well, then," he asked reasonably, "what is the reason I'm not having a cold beer under a palm tree just now?"

"Business. This is business. We had a request for a charter beginning Sunday and uh . . . I've had to book the *Swan,* since there was absolutely nothing else suitable. I realize it's short notice," she added, conversationally retreating from the thundercloud on his brow.

He said nothing.

"Only two people. Honeymooners from Illinois. Midwesterners are awfully nice—not too pushy; open, friendly. And strong. They'll be a great help. Say something, will you?" she demanded, exasperated.

"No."

"No, what?"

"No, thank you. I won't take the charter. And if you ever book another without checking with me first, I'll take your desk apart, pencil by pencil, and send it and your vaulting ambition back to Newport on the next train."

"Boat."

"Whatever."

"Listen to me, Captain," she warned, finding her courage at last. "The owner of your yacht made it available for charter. This"—she slammed the calendar on the desk—"is your very empty charter schedule. You cannot turn away clients when they're silly enough to offer hard cash for the pleasure of enduring your insufferable arrogance for a week."

"So sue me."

"Damn it, I . . . I will." She riffled through his file, seeing absolutely nothing in her mounting fury. "Who's the owner of the *Swan*, anyway?"

"I am."

She looked up at him, dumbfounded, and bit her lower lip to hide her surprise. "Oh, no. Oh . . . hell."

"You won't find my name in the file," he said quietly. "I hide behind the corporate barricade of Swan, Inc. It keeps the opportunists at bay. And if they come swimming up to me like lemmings tomorrow," he added, "I'll know whom to thank."

"How . . . really, how dare you. You can take your *Swan* and *stuff* it, Captain." And she marched out the door.

Thirty seconds later, she marched in again. "This is *my* office," she announced regally.

"And you'd like it back? Of course." He exhaled slowly. "I guess it's *mañana*, then."

"Don't count on it."

"If the rest of your cooking is as exciting as these hors d'oeuvres, our honeymooners are in for a real treat." Leda smiled reassuringly.

The varnished wood of the *Lorna Doone* glowed in the slanted rays of the setting sun, and the pink-and-green sky throbbed with carnival vibrancy. The island was even more beautiful viewed from the cockpit of a boat than from her cottage. Hilly little Bequia with its New England houses might have been Rhode Island, except for the palm trees, the brilliance of the colors, and the balmy evening air. Except for the *Swan*, anchored a hundred feet away from them.

"This will be our first charter ever," the young girl admitted nervously. "Or possibly I shouldn't have said that." Carol looked at her husband. "Should I have said that?"

"Sure, why not." Sam laughed. "Maybe it'll get us the sympathy vote. Anything to pay the mortgage."

"The *Lorna Doone* is beautiful belowdecks, Sam. I'd never have guessed . . . ," Leda began.

". . . seeing her from the outside? I know, I know; that's why we're painting the hull. You sure you don't mind helping us, Leda? Saturday's your day of rest, isn't it?"

"I'll rest on Sunday, after you're on your way with the honeymooners."

"Okay, then, here's the plan. Carol catches the dawn ferry to St. Vincent for groceries, and you and I start painting at seven, before the trade winds pipe up. I'll pick you up at the dinghy dock. Wear old clothes; I'm a sloppy painter."

On Saturday mornings the harbor slept in. Leda stood all alone on the dock, obligingly dressed in a pair of ragged cutoffs and an old halter top.

C'mon, c'mon, Sam; let's get moving. Already gentle breezes were beginning to ruffle the surface of the harbor. Where was he, anyway? On the other hand, it was his boat; why should she care if the paint job didn't turn out smooth as glass?

You're getting too manic for your own good, Sayers. Slow it down. Right now she was tapping her foot. How absurd; she wasn't a foot tapper. Had he said why he couldn't take the charter? He'd said, "No, thank you." Probably he didn't do newlyweds; starry-eyed wives would be tough nuts to crack.

"Sam! Why on earth are you rowing? Is the outboard engine dead?"

"Well, no," he said sheepishly. "But it's pretty early; I didn't want to wake up the harbor."

She jumped into the dinghy with a surprised smile. "Do you have any idea how nice you are?"

" 'Nice' is my stock in trade. Some make it on looks; I make it on nice."

60

His face did have a kind of offbeat appeal: earnest brown eyes; comic Adam's apple; lazy crooked-tooth smile. He was night-and-day different from the handsome intensity of his neighbor Nat Hardy. The phrase "no, thank you" had probably never entered Sam Connor's head.

"So who paints? You or me or both?" She was as eager as a puppy.

"Uh, no offense, but I think I'll do the painting. I've done it before."

"So have I," she answered indignantly.

He rolled his eyes. "Oh, sure—back porches and kitchen walls."

"*Yachts,* mister. I can do it."

"Well, I'll do the starboard side while you hold the dinghy away from the *Doone.* Then you can take a shot at the port side. We'll see how it goes."

"And the better painter gets treated to a planter's punch," she demanded fearlessly.

"Okay, why not."

An hour later the breeze was up, the sun was up, and so was Sam's temper.

"Damn! The paint's drying as fast as I lay it on; I may as well be painting with biscuit batter."

"You're right, Sam," she said soothingly. "These conditions stink." She was well on her way to a first-rate sunburn, unless paint splatters were an adequate sunscreen. Her arms shook from the effort of holding the dinghy steady, and a fierce crick had settled permanently in the small of her back. She decided that all in all, painting was probably easier.

"Okay, your turn. You can't do any worse than this," Sam said disgustedly. "Let's ease the dinghy to the other side."

They moved to the port side. Poised with brush in hand, Leda took a deep breath and prepared to plunge.

A voice rang through the air. "Ahoy there, Wonder Woman! Is there anything you *can't* do?"

Oh, no. Not here. Not now. Nat Hardy was standing in the

cockpit of his boat, arms akimbo, a friendly grin flashing through his black beard.

"I can't talk and paint at the same time, for one thing," she yelled back, and she laid down the first stroke of paint. She was surprised to see him on deck so early. Juanita looked like the coffee-in-bed type. And that was all the reflection Leda had time for, because she had to paint as fast as humanly possible to keep a wet edge going. Her wrist and middle fingers began to ache unbearably.

"Dinghy's too close to the hull, Sam," she gasped between strokes.

"Hmmm? Oh, sorry. Guess I wasn't paying attention."

"Well, pay some, then," she said shortly. She stole a quick glance at his face. "What're you gawking at?"

"Her. Geez. She does that every morning. Carol usually makes me stay belowdecks around this time, fixing the wiring or sorting out the bad potatoes, or something."

On the deck of the *Swan,* Juanita—and Nat—were finishing up deep knee bends and moving on to sit-ups. She in a bikini, he in khaki shorts. How very healthy of them. *I've got to finish and get out of here,* Leda thought desperately.

"Sam! The dinghy's bumping the hull."

"Yeah . . . right. Oh, wow. What's it called when you're on your hands and one knee and you . . . let's see . . . bring your other foot toward your bottom?"

"Donkey kicks—which is what you'll be feeling if you don't hold this dinghy off."

"Not to worry, you're doing splendidly," he allowed kindly.

Leda had beaten Sam's time by about fifteen minutes. Exhausted, she extricated her paint-sticky hand from the paintbrush and halfheartedly began cleaning herself up with a turpentined rag. "I'm a mess, Sam. I don't dare go aboard your boat. Can you just take me back ashore?" ·

"Yep. Just let me dump these brushes in a can of thinner."

A small boat nudged their dinghy from behind. "I'll take care of the lady for you, Sam," came the now familiar voice.

"Hey, thanks, Nat. I'll catch you later, Leda. Looks like the rum punches are on me," he added wryly. "Trust a girl to make a fool of a man."

For the second time since her arrival, Leda found herself in Nat's runabout. "The inevitable Captain Hardy. I think I liked you better the first time you kidnapped me," she said, scowling.

"Careful—flattery makes me dizzy. Your side of the hull turned out rather well," he added amiably.

"Watch it—flattery makes *me* suspicious," she returned.

"I've noticed that. Would you feel more reassured if I said, for instance, that you looked like an old shoe?"

She looked down at her paint-splattered cutoffs and grimaced. "Probably not. That's the trouble with paranoids. Well, the paint has cured and my rag has dried," she said resignedly. "I'll probably look like an apprentice handyman for the rest of the winter."

"Under your seat there's a bottle of mineral spirits you can use to clean up," he volunteered.

"Well, well, the complete host," she said, upside-down and searching. "Where're the olives?"

"For external use only, lass. However, I do stock the internal kind of spirits on the *Swan* if you're interested," he said, raising and lowering his eyebrows in Groucho-Marx lechery.

"I'm *not.*" They climbed onto the dock, and Leda avoided looking at him as she scrubbed her arms clean of paint. Obviously he was a lunatic. Did he seriously think he could ply her with liquor, with Juanita manning—wrong word—the cocktail shaker? Leda knew nothing of life in the fast lane, really. How could he think she was capable of such blatant sexuality? It was insulting. Her eyes smarted, perhaps from the paint thinner.

"Give me that rag; the backs of your thighs are as white as a dairy barn." Nat poured a little thinner over the rag and began, gingerly, to rub the paint away, in full view, of course, of everyone in Admiralty Bay. "Can't we do the mopping up somewhere else?" she asked, resisting an urge to put her hands over her face and hide.

"My sentiments precisely. Your place or—not to seem a bore about it—mine?"

63

"Captain, has it occurred to you that *your* place is already occupied?"

"Occu— Juanita? So what?" he asked blankly. "I'm just going to clean you up and cool you off, not tie you to the mast and ravage you. Spread your legs apart."

"Oh, sure. Captain Kidd's words exactly. *Yow.* That thinner burns." He had worked his way to her inner thighs, and the sensitive, unexposed skin was far more tender than her arms had been. Very, very gently he dabbed at the paint spots, leaving a hot trail higher and higher—and higher—up her thigh.

Recipe for a bonfire: some flammable paint thinner, the fiery Hardy touch, and a pinch of profound embarrassment. Her cheeks flamed.

"I could see this if I were Joan of Arc," she grumbled. "Are you planning to set a torch to me when you've finished?"

"Joan of Arc. You know, that's not a bad comparison, actually. Same pluck, same militancy, same virginal innocence," he added meaningfully. He stood up. "There, you're done."

So that was how he interpreted her reluctance the other night. "Virginal innocence." Naturally. Who else but a determined virgin could resist the formidable powers of Nathan Hardy? Ha. Very easy on his ego, that theory. Well, he had presumed too much, this time. She would not be taken for an innocent—virginal or otherwise. Nat Hardy wasn't the only one with experience. Just because she hadn't jumped into bed when he snapped his fingers, it didn't mean she was a saint. Dammit. "I am not an innocent, Captain."

"Ah, well, I won't argue. How about an early lunch?"

She turned back to him in amazement. "Not a chance."

"Maybe a little windsurfing, then? I've got two sailboards."

"I'd sooner wrestle with an alligator," she snapped.

He dabbed imperturbably at a paint speck on her right cheek. "Okay, this is your last chance. As it happens, I have an inspired recipe for blackfish stew—and the necessary blackfish as well. All *you* have to supply tonight is the hot plate. Is that asking so much?"

With that orphan smile, he ought to be in fund-raising, she

decided warily. "It's asking way too much. *No.*" Help. She couldn't hold out much longer.

"Y'know, I'm damned sorry I ever warned you about keeping your guard up down here," he said, suddenly annoyed. "Don't you think you're overdoing it a bit?"

"I'm not keeping anything up, Captain—least of all, any further conversation with you. If you'll excuse me," she said, sniffing, "I have charters to take care of."

"Aha! So you're still sulking over the charter I turned down." He took her by the shoulders, which were still tender and stinging from the paint solvent. The callused, sinewy strength of his sailor's hands thrummed into her consciousness, despite the lightness of his grasp. High voltage, high voltage, high voltage . . . Keep away. Leda whipped around, freeing herself from him; the broken contact allowed something deep inside her to snap.

"The one thing in the world we're *not* talking about is that stupid charter. Didn't you know that I could replace you like . . . like that?" She snapped her fingers imperiously.

"So, you've replaced me just"—he snapped his fingers mockingly—"like that." They were still on the little dinghy dock, and a small boat puttered up with a giggling couple aboard; they tied up their dinghy, gave Leda and Nat a curious look, and sauntered away. Nat lowered his voice. "What the devil *are* we arguing about, then?" he growled.

Leda sat down on the edge of the wooden dock and dangled her feet in the warm water. Oh, she knew, even if he didn't, what it was about.

Nat had crouched down beside her like a baseball catcher, his forearms crossed and dangling over his solid thighs. Curiosity and expectation emanated from him. "Well?"

"We're arguing, obviously, about your inconsistency." It had been eating at her for days. Now she'd said it, and she was glad.

"Good of you to put it so precisely for me," he said dryly. "Unfortunately, I don't know what in hell you're talking about."

"You want me to spell it out for you? Dot every *i*, cross every *t* in *inconsistent?* All right, then. Didn't you tell me, the other night, that you'd never take a woman to sea?" She forced her eyes to meet his.

His look was blank. "Yes?"

"Well, what's Juanita . . . chopped liver?" It was the first time Leda ever said the name aloud, and she felt strangely guilty, as if she'd sworn in front of her father. In spite of herself, her lower lip trembled.

Nat said nothing for a moment. He was thinking quickly, and on more levels than one, that was obvious. If Leda had had to describe his look in a courtroom, she'd have said it combined surprise with amusement, wariness, and maybe a little sadness.

"Juanita," he said steadily, "is exactly what she seems to be —my crewmember. No more, no less. She does the cooking and cleaning and helps me with sail-handling. She's extremely attractive and personable, and my charter guests like that. So do I."

Leda jumped to her feet, mortified and yet strangely elated. "No more, no less," he'd said.

"But you said you'd never take a woman—"

"—to sea. I meant across oceans for weeks, a month at a time. Puddle-jumping on charter trips between these islands is not going to sea in my book. You don't go to sea with a bit of fluff like Juanita, or, as I think I've made clear, with *any* woman. I hope I've cleared up any questions about my . . . consistency," he said with a wry smile.

Abashed, Leda fiddled with a hanging thread on her denim cutoffs. "Well, obviously it makes no difference to me one way or the other. I was just . . . curious."

He reached down and brought the back of her hand up to his lips. She'd never noticed before how small her own rather capable hand seemed, inside his. Her heartbeat had become audible; surely he must hear it too. Surging adrenaline spread like wildfire through her veins, making her light-headed. It seemed to Leda that her feelings, her thoughts, and her body had all been brutally exposed to Nat and the rest of the harbor as they stood alone in the blinding sun. He was driving her quite mad.

"About Juanita," he began with a friendly smile. "Don't think for a minute that I mistook your curiosity for jealousy. Jealousy wouldn't have been consistent with your refusal to take me up on any of my offers."

"Jealousy?" she said vaguely. "Oh, no, that wouldn't be consistent at all."

He looked at her, she looked at him back, and before he turned to go he said, "There's not much point in my hanging around Bequia, then. See you next week sometime, boss."

"Delighted, I'm sure."

Just like that? Gone? Lock, stock, and Juanita? Leda couldn't write, she couldn't call, she couldn't say, "Ask me one more time"? Heartless gypsy! This is what it meant, then, to be attracted to a sailor. In ten minutes Nat Hardy, all his earthly belongings, and his Brazilian sidekick would be sailing off into the Caribbean sunset. Why couldn't he work in an office, like ordinary people? Truck drivers, traveling salesmen, foreign diplomats—all of them at least had a home to come back to. She was suddenly crushed by the thought of Juanita doing domestic little chores on the *Swan,* like baking bread or washing dishes.

Oh damn, damn, *damn.* She was jealous. She ached all over, inside and out, with jealousy. How had it come to this? She was jealous of a woman who wasn't even his. He'd said that; there was that comfort, at least. But . . . A week? With her? Alone on a boat? So what if he'd considered her merely a "bit of fluff." Bits of fluff were probably good in bed. Still, at least Nat didn't admire Juanita for her mind. Yippee.

Oh damn, damn, damn. Could a person be so jealous if she weren't . . . falling in love?

CHAPTER FOUR

It was time to rearrange the furniture. Leda had done everything she could possibly think of to while away the week, and the only thing left was rearranging the furniture. On Saturday, after she'd sat desolated on the side of a grassy hill watching Nat and . . . Fluffy . . . sailing out of the harbor, she stayed holed up in her cottage, moping and pining. On Sunday, all day, more moping, more pining. On Monday evening she read, or at least turned the pages of, a book. Tuesday she worked late, straightening out the filing system. Wednesday. On Wednesday she mended all her clothes, for Pete's sake! She *hated* mending. And anyway, mending left her mind too free to speculate.

Thursday wasn't too bad; that was barbecue night at the Frangipani. She'd met dozens of people, and when someone clanged the dinner bell for the second seating, it was Leda who was among the first in line for the huge buffet and hot-sauced steak. Nat would've been amused to see that pining hadn't affected her appetite, at any rate. On Friday she'd been asked to dinner by the captain of one of the few yachts that wasn't being frantically prepared for a Christmas charter. She refused; captains made rotten dinner dates, all things considered. Wine you, dine you, see you in a week, boss.

Well, a week ended yesterday. In her office, where she really had been busy all day, Leda lost countless arguments with herself over whether she should look out at the harbor for new arrivals or not. Plenty of boats sailed into Admiralty Bay on Saturday, but none so lofty, none so handsome, none so longed, for, as Captain Hardy's *Swan*.

And now it was Sunday. Awakened by the peal of the bronze

bell—their bell—in the Anglican church, Leda had managed to drag herself wearily through the sleepy island day. So very little happened on a Sunday. Bequians, like Americans, took their families to play on the beaches. A new flock of tourists settled happily into the guest houses and lounge chairs at Coco's. Most of the yachts sailed out with their charter parties for a whirl-wind week-long tour of the half-dozen tiny islands nearby.

Whoever wasn't sailing or swimming or sunning, was wind-surfing. Half a dozen young men, and one or two young women, were showing off their agility—and their physiques—as they stood on the sail-driven boards, gliding gracefully back and forth across the harbor. By the time Leda decided once and for all to shake herself free of her low spirits, trot down to the beach, and try her hand at windsurfing, the sun was going down and everyone was hauling his or her windsurfer out of the water and heading to the Rum-Dum for sundowners. Somehow Leda couldn't get excited about drinking rum punches and watching the sun go down with a bunch of beach boys, and so she wandered back to her cottage.

That left the furniture. Not that there was much to move around, in a cottage fifteen feet wide and eighteen feet long. But Leda was a great bedtime reader, and a nightstand to hold a cup of tea was an absolute necessity. She had plundered the rental cottages methodically, and her booty lay piled near the door: a rickety oval-shaped bedstand from the Yellow Cottage; a rather pretty braided rug from the Purple Cottage (Julie *did* tell Leda to take whatever she needed); and her most sensational find, a vividly rendered chalk drawing of Admiralty Bay by an un-known hand. The proportions were all wrong (Port Elizabeth was right where Princess Margaret Beach should have been), but the effect was pure, joyous carnival.

Leda squeezed the wobbly little table next to the bed, but it bumped up against the louvered folding screen that partitioned off the sleeping area. She moved the screen a little. Now it bumped into the overstuffed, floral-patterned couch. There was definitely no place for the couch to go; maybe she should just get rid of the folding screen. *After all,* she told herself, *you live like a hermit; why should you want privacy?* She fiddled with the partition, trying to make everything fit.

"Open this door or I'll blow the damn thing down!"

He was back; her heart turned over, and her head, for some odd reason, began to pound. "Ca-aptain. Is that you?" she croaked, dashing to her radio to turn down the calypso music that blared cheerfully over the airwaves.

"Who do y'think it is, the Big Bad Wolf?" he growled on the other side of the door.

An absurd, uncontrollable cheek-splitting grin lit her face as she opened the door to him. "If the fur fits . . ." she intoned, her eyes glittering with mischief.

He had a rum punch in each hand—well, half a rum punch in each hand—and he looked bigger, broader, more tanned and handsome than she'd remembered. He looked . . . *real.*

He handed Leda one of the punches. "Drink it. The other half is spilled on the step path where I tripped in the dark. The other half of mine is spilled all over my arm, which is what happens when you try to knock on the door with your elbow. I also tried calling your name and kicking the door with my foot." He moved over to the sink, rolled the sleeves of his muslin safari shirt over his elbows, and ran water up and down the length of his sticky forearm. "Damn radio; you sounded like a blasted teenager in here."

"I like calypso; it's happy music," she said, trying to wipe off the smile that was still stuck to her face.

"Good. Maybe you'll be more civil to me tonight. Finish that drink and change," he ordered, walking over to her little closet. He reached in and pulled out the backless dress with the little coral flowers. "You can wear this one."

"Not that one," she said instantly. "What is this all about, anyway?"

"We're going to the jump-up at the Sunny Caribee. What about this, this black gauzy bit, then?"

"That's my best dress! I'm saving it," she argued. What she was saving it for, she had no idea.

70

"Well, you can't go in those shorts and that rag of a shirt," he said with a withering look. "Finish your drink."

"I haven't even had supper yet," she protested, draining the punch in one intimidated gulp.

He was looking around. "Ah. The very thing." He cleared the top of a large tattered trunk, which Leda was using as a coffee table, and removed a bright piece of red-and-orange batik fabric that she'd thrown over it. He held the square of cloth between his outstretched arms. "Ever worn a pareu before?" he asked her.

"You mean, a sarong?"

"I mean, a pareu. In the Caribbean it's called a pareu. They say there're a dozen different ways to tie 'em, but all I know is one. Take off your clothes."

"You're crazy." Her eyes opened wide. The potent drink went racing through her limbs, and she thought that perhaps she ought to sit down.

Instead, Nat wrapped the piece of batik around her, over her shorts, and over her blouse. "Right, then; what you'll do is grab each end like this and fold the material under to form a sort of . . . of . . . ," he groped.

"Pleat."

"A pleat . . . and then tie the corners in a square knot in front, and you'll be right as rain. Got it?"

"Oh, yes, I've got it, all right." She giggled suddenly. *I've got it bad.* He was wearing after-shave. She'd never known him to wear after-shave before. She inhaled deeply and raised herself up on her bare toes. "After-shave? 'Snice."

Nat gave her an appraising look, spun her around, and aimed her at the louvered screen. "Change."

The half-spin nearly put Leda into orbit. "Oh *my;* that punch packs a . . . punch," she whispered.

Behind the screen she unzipped her shorts and tossed them over the divider. Her blouse was trickier to manage; the little mother-of-pearl buttons had a way of slithering out of her fingers. But at last it, too, got thrown over the divider. She slipped on a pair of low-cut underpants. *Now* for the hard part. Wrap-

71

ping the hot-colored cotton around her tan body, Leda formed two pleats before trying to join the ends in a square knot. Her brow wrinkled in fierce concentration. "To make the square knot," she muttered uncertainly, "you go left over right and then you go left over . . . or is that . . . no wait, start over. You go left . . . right . . ."

"Leda," Nat said patiently from the other side of the screen.

"Yes? Nat?"

"Left over right, right over left."

"I knew that." She took a deep breath and stared at the ends. She hadn't the faintest idea how to make a square knot looking downward; it was pointless to try. She clutched the ends of the fabric in her fists close to her breast and came out from behind the screen, walking with little geisha steps. "I can't."

Nat gave her a long, long look. The barest, subtlest hint of a smile curved his mouth; or maybe the smile was in his blue eyes. Wherever it came from, his look was so soft, so dear, that Leda's white-knuckled grip on the fabric went limp, and the cloth nearly fell to the floor. "Oops," she whispered moronically, embarrassed by her loss of coordination.

"Leda Sayers, under the influence," he murmured in a low voice as he took the fabric ends from her. "Who'd have reckoned it?"

"I am *not* under the influence of *any*thing," she intoned as she blinked down at the dazzling bright batik in his sun-darkened hands. "I just haven't eaten for a while."

"That, I find hard to believe." He laughed as he pulled the fabric away from her to center the opening along the entire front of her body.

She froze before him, naked and befuddled. Well, *nearly* naked, *practically* befuddled. She was certainly at his mercy now. He had her just where he wanted her. How utterly stupid of her to play into his hands this way. A wild sense that she'd reached a moment of crisis, one she'd remember for the rest of her life, overwhelmed her. The hot red-and-orange pattern of the cloth leaped into fireballs of flame that danced in the air between them. It would be idiocy to resist; even greater idiocy to submit.

"Left over right, right over left. See how simple?" Nat tied the ends firmly across her breasts, adjusted the knot, smoothed her long hair, and said, "Get your sandals. We're going dancin'."

For dancing, Bequia was the place to be. Night after night, calypso music from a steady stream of steel-drum bands, combos (and when all else failed, stereo records) reverberated across the basin-shaped harbor. Night after night, Leda had been tempted to follow the Pied-Piper sound of calypso into the Frangipani, or the Sunny Caribee, or the Old Fig Tree. But who wanted to go to a jump-up alone?

Once or twice during the last week she'd played her two calypso records, closed her eyes, and pretended she was dancing with—or at least, next to—Nat. People rarely danced in one another's arms at Bequia's casual jump-ups; that much she'd learned, before she slipped away from the lively sounds of the combo that played after Thursday's barbecue at the Frangipani.

But it was Sunday now, and the haunting, melodic sounds of the steel-drum band pulsed through Leda's body as she danced with happy abandon under the stars at the Sunny Caribee. The dance area was small and overflowing with a whole range of talent—from cool, rhythmic Bequians who took their calypso seriously, to stiff-legged resort guests who would need several more rum punches before they could, in the language of calypso, "roll their bumbulums" with any confidence.

As a couple, Leda and Nat fell somewhere in the middle. Despite his competence, Nat was not a showstopper on the dance floor; he was too blasé, too detached. Leda chalked it up to British reserve. *She,* on the other hand, was feeling perfectly splendid. The pareu made her feel unbelievably provocative. Perhaps it was the way the material bound her breasts; or the way it fluttered open in the front when she got near the edge of the dance floor and the trade winds caught and lifted the airy fabric. Whatever the reason, she felt exotic and intensely feminine.

And giddy. Nat had managed to wheedle a sandwich for

73

Leda out of the barkeep, even though dinner was no longer being served; the solid food and the fresh night air had a sobering effect on Leda—for a while. But before long, she was tipsy all over again, on stars and palm trees, the drum music, and Nat's amused laughter. It was the most heavenly time she'd ever known. She was unbearably tantalized by having Nat so near, yet so safely at a distance. There was something in the simple, driving beat that made her drag Nat out onto the dance floor again and again. She simply could not get enough of the music.

She swayed, she swung her hips, she *moved* for Nat. She really couldn't help it; it was part of the spell. Her senses were being assaulted on every side by the incredible beauty of the Caribbean experience—by sweet floral perfume and husky male exertion; by kaleidoscopic colors on dark-skinned Bequians, and flashing, singing laughter all around her; by the feel of the timeworn wooden dance floor under her now bare feet; and most of all, by the almost overpowering energy of the steel drums, which she had drawn closer and closer to in her dancing, until she felt as though the notes were being played on her own body. She was helpless; it was part of the spell.

When the players broke for an intermission, she collapsed into a lounge chair, deliriously happy—and thirsty. Once again, a tall, icy rum punch appeared magically at her place; the tart blend of citrus and passion-fruit juices soothed her dry throat as nothing else had ever done.

"Where are these divine drinks all coming from?" she asked Nat, dangling her fifth maraschino cherry by the stem and biting into it.

"Where, indeed," he returned, glancing around their table. They were sitting with five or six other yachtspeople. "I think Sam bought this last round."

Nat was leaning back in a white metal lawn chair, looking at Leda as if he were an artist studying his latest work from a new perspective. "So. Inside my little Leda was a Dorothy Lamour, just itching to break loose," he mused, playing absentmindedly with the end of his mustache.

"Dorothy Lamour?"

"You've never seen *Road to Rio?*"

" 'Course, I have. What do *you* know about Dorothy Lamour? You're British." Her tone was lofty.

"I have a videocassette library aboard the *Swan.* Naturally," he added dryly, "I'm partial to tropical films."

"Ah, yes . . . the idle rich." She nodded, secretly staggered by his nonchalance; a videocassette library on a *boat?* "So tedious, to be fighting boredom all day long," she said. "Personally, I'm rather partial to Abbott and Costello movies," she finished up breezily. "Shall we dance?" She stood up, and the Caribbean made a quick revolution around her head before settling back into place again.

Nat took the cherry stem from her empty glass and added it to a little pile of stems in an ashtray. Well! He was . . . he was keeping track!

"The drums aren't beating anymore, Miss Lamour, or hadn't you noticed?"

"Oh, yes. Of course. I just meant, shall we . . . walk?"

"Now, that is the first sensible idea you've had since I came up with the insane one of coming here in the first place." He groaned, pulling himself up out of his chair with an effort. "I haven't danced so much since . . . I haven't danced so much, period," he said grimly.

The band was loading their steel drums into a truck. The throbbing, lyrical instruments, Leda could see, were really common, ordinary oil drums. Some were whole; some were cut in half. All were, despite their bright blue paint, a little rusty. She wanted to beg the band, *pay* the band, to set the drums up again and fill the night with their magical beat. Was it really over?

No—it wasn't! Someone had put on a calypso record, and the loudspeakers had begun blaring a new wave of energy through Leda and most of the other dancers.

"Nat—one more! Oh, *please,* just one more."

His smile was half weary, half amused. "One, and *only* one, Miss Lamour. After that I shall haul you offstage by your long hair if I have to."

How very unreasonable he was being. Anyone could see that dancing was what people were meant to do in the Caribbean. The record was a popular one and the lyrics, as in most calypso songs, were sly and witty. The punch line involved the little-known fact that there were *three* rings in a wedding: the wedding rings, and the suffer-ring.

Nat's sudden loud laugh was unexpected and entirely good-natured. The British reserve dropped away, and he bounced and bumped and ground away with Leda and the remaining core of dancers. When the song ended, he applauded as heartily as everyone else.

"One more?" she said with a tragic look and a tiny voice.

"Home."

She was exhausted, it was true. But who cared? The Caribbean was *won*derful. Bequia was *won*derful. Nat was *won*derful. They were walking hand-in-hand down a very dark path that opened out into a small street. Every so often, Leda would burst into a little dance, still spellbound. Why couldn't she act *used* to it, like the other strollers who were ahead of them, the ones who'd turned around when they heard Leda humming and singing, and laughed at her?

"I s'pose you find me embarralasing . . . embarras-sing-ly provincial, don't you," she announced grandly. "You being a Londoner and all," she added, to clear up any doubts.

"I think you're refreshing," he whispered softly, freeing her hand, slipping his arm around her waist and drawing her close to him.

"Oh sure; the little bimbo from Bangor." Her sigh was melodramatic. "Well, we can't *all* be sophisticated ladies from London and Rio," she said profoundly.

"Much better to be a free spirit," he agreed.

"Is it. Is it *really*," she sniffed. He wasn't supposed to agree with her.

Automatically, they stopped at the gate to the little Anglican Church. Leda stared intently at the bronze church bell. "Yep. I think I'll just ring that bell. Free spirits can do that, you know," she threatened with a sideways look at Nat.

76

"You won't ring that bell," he said calmly.

"Yes, I will. It's what bells are for. To ring." She opened the gate and tiptoed into the churchyard and up to the heavy bronze bell, which, close up, seemed enormous and towering. She turned around to look at Nat, who was leaning with forearms folded casually over the gate, his hands locked together loosely. Obviously he didn't believe her.

"Okay, Nat." She grabbed the thick bellpull in both hands and looked at him; he was still smiling. "Guess the answer: Will this ring be 'de wed-ding ring, or de suffer-ring'?" she quoted, giggling and overcome with a sense of her own brilliance.

Several Bequian men and women, also returning from the dance, were walking past. "She goin' to ring dat bell, mon," one of them said to Nat.

Nat shook his head. "She won't ring the bell," he answered with irritating confidence.

"Oh, she won't, will I?"

BON-N-N-N-G-G!

On the way back to her cottage, chastened and with her ears still ringing, Leda said in an awestruck voice, "The devil must have made me do it, Nat."

"Devil drink, you mean," he said imperturbably.

"I don't know *what* I mean," she said, moaning. "Did anyone see me?"

"I should think so; I saw the curtains in the rectory move just before you tore out of the yard."

"Oh-h, no, don't tell me that. Even if it's true, don't tell me, not tonight."

"And what's so special, Miss Lamour, about tonight?"

They were at the bottom of the step path to Leda's cottage. Visibility, as usual when there was no moon, was zero.

"Tonight? Tonight! What's so special about tonight is, it's the first time I've felt completely, totally . . . *me,*" she cried, standing on the bottom step. "Do you know that song?" she asked suddenly. " 'I've Got to Be Me'?"

Nat was standing just below Leda, eye-level with her. He shook his head. "I'm afraid I missed that one."

"Oh, right. You're British. How veddy awkward," she mimicked. "The cultural gap, dash it all. Anyway, I don't remember all the words but it goes, something, something, I've got to be *me,* something, something, got to beee *me-e-e,*" she sang the Sinatra hit, throwing out her arms in an imitation of Barbra Streisand, and whirling around dramatically to climb the next step. "Oof! *Ow,*" she yelped. "Oh, my *toe.*"

"Miss Lamour, allow me," Nat said with elaborate courtesy, and scooped her up in his arms as if she were a sack of corn.

It was surprisingly nice, to be scooped up. Not that she'd had much experience, but it did seem to Leda that she fit the contours of Nat's broad, hard chest like a soft kid glove. No shifting of her weight was necessary; no tweaking or fine-tuning or pounding of the pillow, so to speak. She just . . . fit.

"I only have one sandal in my hand." She sighed happily.

"I know; the other one went flying into the bushes on the last note of your swan song. We can look for it tomorrow, in the daylight." Up they went, step by step, closer and closer to the stars, and to Leda's cottage.

Did he say *"You* can look" or *"We* can look" for the sandal in the daylight? *What a difference a pronoun makes,* she thought longingly. Her cheek was nestled against his shoulder; her arms were around his neck. With each step they took, the soft pareu slid another half inch, exposing more and more of her thigh. It would've seemed prudish to tuck the fabric back, and so she left it alone; but she did notice that her leg seemed suddenly very long.

"My toe's stopped hurting," she whispered, nestling closer.

"Toes will do that," he answered in a low murmur. He made no effort to stand Leda back on her feet.

She drank in the scent of him, and the stars in the sky seemed to drop down inside her head. "Naturally I can walk the rest of the way myself."

"Naturally." He kissed her right temple once, and then again.

"On the other hand, why bother?" she rambled dreamily. "This is more fun."

"*I* thought so," he agreed as they reached her door. It wasn't locked, of course, and he opened it and carried Leda into the cottage. The red-shaded table lamp threw a warm glow over the interior, and Leda noticed for the first time that the colors of her newly acquired chalk drawing seemed psychedelic. Or was that the rum? In the meantime, she was still in Nat's arms, and he was carrying her to the other end of the room, behind the louvered partition, and laying her on the bed.

Bending over her, he held her flushed cheeks between his hands and looked at her with questioning urgency. "Leda . . ." he began in a husky voice.

She bit her lower lip and returned his look as steadily as she was able. "Aye, sir?"

"Are you still interested in 'being you' tonight?"

"Well . . ." Well, she wasn't sure what he meant by that. She thought she knew, but he wasn't being very specific. She flopped her arms open wide on the bed. The pareu had drifted off to the left, off to the right, and her legs lay mostly exposed. "Yes," she said simply, with a smile that was quite timid compared to the provocative position she had unwittingly assumed.

"Are you sure, Miss Lamour?" His smile was heart-melting.

Why did he keep trying to make it an intellectual decision on her part? Why didn't he just take her in his arms and . . . take her? The sight of him standing above her made the bed begin to spin around—she really must have the bed checked—and she raised her arms to him. "Captain?" she asked tentatively.

He lowered himself onto the bed until he was lying against her full length, his left leg lying partly over her right. His hand slipped through the long front opening of her pareu, and he began, with long, slow strokes, to trace the outline of the curve from the side of her breast, down to her waist, back out over her hipline, and down the outer length of her thigh. When his arm had reached its full length, he reversed and trailed his hand back up again, until it reached the side of her breast beneath the binding of the pareu.

79

"I've changed my mind about the pareu, incidentally. Some women can wear them; you cannot."

Leda, who had begun to drift off on her flying bed under the slow, arousing circuit he was tracing, fell back to earth. "Izzat so? I thought I looked perfectly fine," she said, her feelings hurt.

"I thought—and so did every other man—that your intention was to incite a riot. Where did you learn to dance like that?"

Mollified, she smiled a sweet, dreamy smile. "I haven't danced since high school. I was just trying to imitate everyone else."

His laugh was low and sensual as he gently raked his hand through a tangle in the shimmering strands of her long golden hair. Twisting a strand around his finger, he tugged gently, setting off a chain reaction of tingling pleasure in the nerve endings of her scalp. His mouth came down on hers slowly and deliberately, and Leda found herself raising her head slightly to hasten the meeting of their lips. The first kiss was deep, satisfying, nothing like the sweet samplers she had enjoyed as he carried her up the path. Again the strange mixture of cheroot, prickly beard, and silver sweetness invaded her mouth, and she knew she was probably ruined forever from enjoying any other man's kiss. *This* mouth, *this* tongue, only.

He moved aside the left half of the pareu fabric, which was still tied securely across her top, and exposed the soft pink tip of her left breast. With his middle finger he traced tiny, feather-light circles around the swelling nipple. Leda's breathing came more quickly, and the knotted fabric suddenly seemed unbearably restrictive.

"The whole point of a square knot," he said softly, "is that it's so very easy to untie." He approached the knot rather cautiously, as if Leda were a half-tame, half-wild deer he had come across on a stroll through the woods. When he untied the knot, the bright fabric fell open, and the whiteness of her breasts lay exposed to his wondering, fascinated gaze. Leda was startled;

she had not fully realized, until that moment, how easily she could be . . . undone.

She laughed a small, faraway laugh. "I think you've got *me* all tied up in knots, sailor man." His head came down toward her breast as the fingers of his left hand wound through her hair and cradled the back of her head reassuringly. The fingertips of his right hand were gliding downward on a journey of their own. So much was happening, so many pleasure centers were being tapped. . . .

Everything seemed to be going around in circles: his mouth, circling and kissing her breast; his hand, rubbing her hair in a concentric pattern on the back of her head; his other hand, practiced, specific; and her own hands, which had somehow got underneath his shirt and were wandering in restless rotations on his warm, solid back.

But most of all, the bed . . . The bed really had begun to levitate; it rose up off the floor, and then it began to whirl around in smaller and tighter circles. Soon it would drop into a black hole in space . . . soon it would . . . soon . . . "Ah, Nat." She sighed, waiting with sweet anguish to plunge into that oblivion.

"Leda, you are the most seductive, fascinating little witch," he rasped.

"No, no," she said mistily, *"you're* seductive and . . . oh-h-h . . . you're fanisate . . . fanis . . ."

"Fascinating," he prompted.

"Yes. That. Oh, don't stop," she said with a disappointed moan as Nat withdrew his hand.

"Leda." His voice had moved from its husky register to a more conversational one. "You tipsy little dope; you're three sheets to the wind, still, aren't you?"

"Nonsense; I'm one hunnerd percent . . . levelheaded." Or at least she would be, as soon as the bed stopped spinning.

With something between a groan and a sigh, he rolled over onto his side, propped himself up on an elbow, and studied her for a moment. His hand slowly trailed along Leda's creamy skin, from her breasts all the way to her navel. "Sober, hey?" he asked skeptically.

"As a judge." She wished he wouldn't do that; or that, if he *were* going to do that . . .

"All right, then, your honor," he said, kissing her lightly on her forehead, "let's see if you can walk a straight line . . . at least, verbally. Suppose you try saying this fast, three times: 'Big bronze bells break easily.' "

"Tut"—she waved her hand in the air—"nothing to it. Big bonze bells . . . Big bronze brells break . . ." She sighed and flopped over on her stomach, and then became suddenly aware that the batik cloth had not rolled over with her. Leaning on both elbows she manipulated her hair as nonchalantly as she was able, so that it fell over her bare breast. "How many tries do I get?"

He shook his head with a rueful smile. "I could lie next to you and watch you try till the sun comes up—which is approximately how long it's going to take for you to rejoin the planet— but . . ." He swung his legs over the side of the bed and sat there a moment with his back to Leda, a solid study in resolve. Then he turned his head over his shoulder toward her, and reached the palm of his hand to the top of her shining hair, down along the arch of her spine and over the rounded curve of her bottom, where he let his hand lay. Leda watched him with shining green eyes that were becoming brighter behind a glaze of tears. She blinked rapidly two or three times, and the welling subsided.

"But," he repeated, drawing in a breath and holding it before exhaling with cheek-puffing force. "You, darlin', are headed for a major case of conscience in the morning. It's best that I sit this one out," he said softly. "Besides, my ego'd prefer that you remember the . . . connection the next time you saw me."

" 'Course I would, darn you." Her face fell, on her nose, into the paisley bedspread. The most sensible thing seemed to be to close her eyes, shutting out the swirl of remorse that had begun to edge up, relentlessly, into her throat.

He rose up from the bed and stood over her. "My loopy little Leda."

The amused tolerance in his voice annoyed her. "Am I s'posed to say *that* three times fast too?" she muttered into the bed covering.

He lifted a strand of hair and let it drop back down onto her bare back. "Just say good night, darlin'."

"Never."

He understood her cryptic refusal. "Ah. Sorry. Darlin', just say good night," he corrected himself.

"Good. Night."

CHAPTER FIVE

"A Monday in Paradise is still a Monday," Leda groaned to no one in particular as she dropped limply into the padded swivel chair behind her desk and closed her eyes. Never had she known the full fury of a hangover before this. Alcohol was simply not Leda's cup of tea; a cup of *tea* was more her cup of tea. Uncork a bottle of wine under Leda's nose, and she became light-headed. And as for rum . . . !

"Sunny Caribee?" Julie asked politely.

"Yes, oh, lord . . . yes. How did you know?" She wondered whether her voice sounded as fuzzy as her tongue felt.

"I've seen the look before," the older woman answered dryly. "Around here it's known as the Jump-up Syndrome. Although I must say, you do look more shell-shocked than most."

"Shock is exactly the right word. I don't know what's come over me since I arrived at Bequia," Leda said disgustedly, lifting her bare feet up onto the desk and sipping slowly from a cup of coffee. All morning long, bits and pieces of completely unbelievable scenarios had been drifting in and out of what was left of her brain. She stared at her rather well-formed bare feet; suddenly it came to her where the missing sandal had gone. Little Leda One-shoe. It just wasn't possible. One more in an apparently endless series of hot blushes tramped across the bridge of her sun-freckled nose.

In her casual moods, Leda had come to work barefoot before, but now she dropped her feet from the desktop and tucked them demurely underneath; it'd be just her luck that Julie would choose this of all mornings to crack down on the dress code. To make matters worse, the odious refrain, "I've-got-to-be-me," drummed in the back of her head, alternating beats with her headache.

"Julie," she began slowly, "do you think the Caribbean can tell you things about yourself that you'd rather not have known? Important things? Do people sometimes go off the deep end around here?" She hoped desperately that Julie understood what she was getting at; she herself did not.

"Certainly; some people never do adjust to the overwhelming sensuality down here. It's all or nothing with them. But I wouldn't worry too much, dear," she added kindly. "That was your first jump-up, and you seem like the levelheaded sort."

"My head doesn't feel all that level at the moment," Leda answered glumly, rummaging through the papers on her desk to see where she'd left off on Saturday. There were two or three responses to a peppy little ad she'd run in *The New York Times;* those must be answered immediately. Even more pressing, there was a copy deadline for the *Yachting* magazine ad coming up. She was having trouble writing that one; how many different ways could you say "exciting"? Her imagination wandered back to the night before. *Lots of different ways,* she moaned as she felt rather than remembered the thrilling, expert touch of Nat's hands on every nerve center she possessed.

The piercing morning sun had reached the exact height of her eyes as she sat staring at the crossed-out and rewritten ad copy. When she closed her eyes in self-defense, she found herself curled in Nat's arms and ascending the step path to her paisley-covered bed. He'd taken her up, up, and then all around. And after that he'd left her cold. *Don't think about that.* It was the one single thought that she'd mercilessly beaten back all morning into the dungeon of her consciousness. She would *not* let it out into the open air.

"Nat Hardy is an A-one, first-class jerk!" she said aloud, peering at her scribbling.

Julie looked up, startled. "You Americans have the most singular expressions. What's the man done *this* time?"

"Nothing," Leda growled.

How could he do nothing? Just walk away like that? He

broke down her defenses; he asked her what she'd wanted, for God's sake. And then, when she lay there, helpless and under his spell and completely vulnerable, he decided, on second thought . . . what? That she wasn't sexy enough? Eyes the wrong color? Too old? Too young? Too cold? That must be it. He didn't think she was responding adequately to his superior technical skills. She drew several thick, angry lines through "Coco's Yacht Charters—No One Does It Better."

No, she was being stupid. Even in her puzzled fury, Leda could not convince herself that Nat had walked out of her cottage because he was bored. She rewrote the ad headline for the fourth time: "Coco's Yacht Charters—Don't Just Dream About It." Hmm. Oh, the heck with it; it was good enough. She'd mail it. That left the stack of customer inquiries.

"What I cannot understand," Leda muttered to her ever-patient employer, "is why Hardy is bothering with charters at all. He doesn't need the money."

"But according to him, he does enjoy the company," Julie suggested.

"Then he should invite his friends, for heaven's sake. Or doesn't he have any?" Leda asked in scathing tones. "He's just such a damned nuisance. For example, these people," she said, rattling a letter at Julie as though it were a fully dressed man and his wife, "are logical candidates for chartering the *Swan:* a married couple with sailing experience, obviously well bred and intelligent. They should be perfect; the letter certainly is. But I'm inclined to route them toward Sam and Carol's *Lorna Doone,* even though they mention the *Swan* by name. And why? Because, number one, Captain Hardy probably won't feel like having company during the first week in February. And number two: The couple wants to bring its dog, a little Scottish terrier. Not a Doberman, not a Great Dane, not a malamute. A little, tiny terrier. It's a very old dog, they write, and it becomes quite distressed in a kennel. Well, if they want to go to the bother of getting pet import permits and tranquilizers and pet carriers, why shouldn't they be able to bring the terrier? His name is Tippy, by the way. But no, you know very well we're not going

86

to get this charter past Captain Hardy's nose because . . . because they want to bring a terrier." She threw up her hands. "Or yellow toothbrushes. Or whatever. He's just so arbitrary. You just can't predict what he's going to do." And she dropped her head onto the back of her chair and stared at the ceiling, near tears.

"Leda. What's wrong." It was a statement, not a question. "It's Nat, obviously, but what about him?"

Leda rolled her head a little sideways and passed on a shaky little smile to Julie, then looked up at the ceiling again. "I . . . ah . . . seem to have gotten involved, don't ask me why." She bit her upper lip to stop it from trembling. Oh, God, she was going to be melodramatic.

"Oh, my dear. How involved?"

Julie's voice was sympathetic and sorrowful; Leda might just as well have confessed that she was suffering from a mysterious, fatal disease. "How involved?" She shrugged wearily. "Who can say?"

"Now, Leda," Julie began briskly, "don't think twice about it. It's perfectly natural to be attracted to a man as handsome as Nat Hardy. Lots of women are. I certainly wouldn't consider it something to act so mournful over."

"You're right, of course. I'm in the throes of a temporary schoolgirl crush—and a crushing headache. Both will pass. What won't go away are these letters, if I don't get cutting on them."

"What singular expressions!" Julie's laugh was relieved.

Leda didn't know what to do about the couple with the terrier. She was afraid to say no, afraid to say yes. Obviously she'd have to ask the Captain himself; but the only people who'd managed not to disrupt her chaotic Monday morning were six-footers with black beards. Leda wrote herself an ostentatious reminder: "Check with Hardy!!!!!" and attached her note to the terrier letter with a big green plastic clip. Putting the letter aside for the moment, she began answering the next inquiry.

"Leda, for heaven's sake. It's lunchtime and I cannot bear all this typewriter-tapping when I've decided to have lunch at my desk. Go away. Take a nap or something." Julie was midway through a very juicy novel; her desk was the one place at which no one would think of looking for her at midday.

"Very good, Madam," Leda answered with a wry smile, rising from her chair and stretching. "Shall I lock the door on the way out?"

"Please."

Leda lifted the hemline of her pale green overblouse and flopped it up and down three or four times to circulate some air around her torso. Noon meant one thing to her: heat. Still, her headache had subsided and her mood had risen from suicidal to grim, perfect for doing business, and the business attached to the green plastic paper clip was still unresolved.

Not for long, however. She retied the belt of her white muslin drawstring pants—in a bow, not a square knot—pulled her hair into a ponytail behind her head, and marched out the door, locking it and then looking around for a dinghy to borrow. If Mohammed was not going to come to the mountain . . .

She found a dinghy; but now she had to find the *Swan*. Nat had not sailed back to his usual place last night. Scanning the harbor from under the shade of her hand, Leda found the boat anchored in the most popular area of Admiralty Bay, just off the Frangipani Restaurant.

How she'd failed to notice the *Swan* before, she couldn't imagine. If nothing else, she should have *heard* it from her office. There were at least a dozen and a half men and women aboard, having an apparently wonderful time. Lots of screaming and laughing; lots of bikinis; lots of jumping, diving, and pushing into the water. They were too far away for her to pick out Nat and Juanita, but she thought she'd heard Nat's deep laugh carry across the water. There was only one laugh like that in all the world.

A regular flotilla of small craft was tied to the stern of the *Swan:* fast runabouts with large outboards; a rowing skiff with lovely lines; even a windsurfer or two. Party, party, party. Welcome to Bequia and the Ship of . . . Wrecks. Didn't anybody *work* around here? She tried to picture herself rowing up to the yacht and climbing aboard, edging through the riotous merry-makers to their leader, hitching up her haute couture draw-string pants, and saying, "Sir. About this terrier . . ." Ha. "Not bloody likely," as the Captain would say.

All her puffed-up determination suddenly gone, Leda decided to seek the cool, quiet shade of a lounge chair under a palm tree at the Reef, the smallest, most out-of-the-way restaurant on the waterfront. There were only one or two people, whom she didn't know, at the counter-bar. Leda ordered a fish sandwich and a cola and collapsed into one of the chairs, picking at her food unenthusiastically.

What she needed most of all was to shut her eyes. No, what she needed most of all was to shut her ears. Even half a harbor away, she was certain she could hear the incessant laughter aboard the *Swan*. She really couldn't stand it. She put her hands over her ears; but then the damned, idiotic refrain came back: I've got to be me-e-e. . . .

Will the real Leda Sayers please stand up? she asked herself in confusion. Workaholic, or hedonist? She decided that, all things considered, she did not cut the mustard as a hedonist; she would be feeling very uncomfortable if she were one of that crowd aboard Nat's yacht, for example. Which meant that Nat had done the right thing when he passed up an opportunity last night. He knew his own kind; and Leda was merely an intoxicated impostor.

With a sense of hopelessness that bordered on despair, Leda, leaving her lunch half eaten, soon dropped off into a deep hour-long sleep. When she awoke she was refreshed and surprisingly philosophical. *Okay, so you wouldn't be comfortable playing a lead role in* La Dolce Vita. *That doesn't mean that you can't enjoy the simpler pleasures that Bequia has to offer. There's still the sun and the ocean, interesting food and pleasant company. . . . Suppose you take things one day at a time.*

The day passed more tolerably after that, but there was still, by four o'clock, the matter of the Scottish terrier to be resolved. When last Leda looked, the *Swan* had emptied. Of course, they could all be below, having an orgy; Leda had decided that just about anything was possible in the islands. She slipped down to the beach to get a closer look. Nat was aboard; he was fiddling with the bow rail. Juanita was not aboard; she was tearing back and forth across the harbor on a windsurfer. Party, party, party. How could anyone so feminine be so tireless?

Leda watched the tawny beauty maneuver the sailboard with almost offhanded confidence. At one point, Juanita paused on the water to chat with an obviously doting admirer, also on a sailboard. She stood so easily and naturally, the left hand holding the bright blue sail half in the water, half out, the other hand reaching over her head to move a long jet-black strand of hair that clung to her left cheek. They were so close to the shore that Leda could see Juanita's dazzling white teeth and the cut of her emerald-green bikini. She made the very idea of windsurfing so attractive that Leda was seized with a desire to windsurf, not row, out to the *Swan* for the terrier discussion.

Dashing up to her cottage for her bathing suit, she began the process of convincing herself that she knew how to windsurf. After all, she was at least as strong or stronger than Juanita. And Leda was a very quick study. Plus she'd once tried windsurfing in Newport Harbor. Granted, the wind had been blowing only three or four knots at the time. She stopped in her tracks. On her doorstep, like a sling-back Cinderella's slipper, sat her missing sandal. So the Prince had been by, sometime. Who cared. The loud thumping of her heart answered her question.

She slipped into her best and newest bathing suit, a wine-red maillot that plunged rather recklessly down the front and was sculpted, more than cut, deep into her midriff on either side, ending in a swooping semicircle across her bottom. She'd bought it the day before she'd left for the islands; and December selections being what they are in New England, she took the only one that fit . . . more or less.

By the time she'd wheedled the use of a windsurfer from a friend who had quit for the day, Leda truly believed that she was capable of an Olympic-class performance. She waded out knee-deep and climbed onto the board a little hastily in her eagerness to look like an old hand. The board slipped out from under her feet like an ice cube on a waxed floor, and she was thrown on her back with a tremendous splash. She bobbed through the water's surface, shook her hair free of her face, and glared at the board as though it were a frisky pony. *Two can play at this game,* she promised, and climbed back onto the board, much more slowly and cautiously. She was standing. A little wobbly, but standing. Now she had to get the sail up from where it lay in the water. Very, very slowly she pulled on the tether, hand over hand, the mast, boom, and sail that were attached to it looking bigger, taller, scarier, as she brought it all to a vertical position.

Meanwhile, of course, the frisky pony and its rider had been floating quietly downwind, in the direction of the *Swan.* When Leda made a desperate lunge to grab the boom, which was absolutely necessary if she was ever to sail, the resulting splash as she fell back into the water was monumental.

This time Nat noticed her. He was the first thing she saw as she cleared the saltwater from her eyes, and he was laughing. Not a polite smirk but uproarious laughter. Was that all people did aboard the *Swan.* Laugh? He was sitting on the bow of his boat, knees up, no shirt, one hand holding a screwdriver, the other gripping the bow rail, no doubt to keep himself from falling over with laughter.

"I'm sorry," he gasped, looking not the least remorseful. "It's just that I've never seen it done with such flamboyance before," he wheezed. *"Truly* sorry."

Leda had climbed back out of the water and was kneeling on the board, trying to paddle the whole shebang toward Nat. The brisk wind, however, was blowing Leda, the board, and the submerged sail and rig like a piece of flotsam past the *Swan* toward the other end of the harbor.

"I wanted to talk to you, Captain," she said as she floated helplessly out of hearing range of Nat.

He cupped a hand to his ear.

"To talk to you," she shouted. "Business," she added as she

91

looked around quickly to see whether every other yacht was tuned in to this afternoon comedy hour.

He stood up and Leda caught her breath at the sheer seductiveness of his form. He was wearing a black nylon swimsuit cut low in the European fashion, which emphasized the trimness of his waist and the lean hardness of his thighs. She felt a twinge of possessiveness; what ever happened to boxer-style swimsuits?

With one smooth motion he dove into the water and began swimming toward her with powerful, swift strokes. Leda, feeling ridiculously like a damsel in distress, tried to hide her embarrassment by assuming a serene, lotuslike position on the sailboard. She could always tell him she'd been meditating.

He reached her in what seemed like record time. "Move over, water lily," he said, hauling himself up onto the board next to her. His extra weight forced the board nearly below the surface of the water, which sloshed over her thighs and added to her sensation of sinking, sinking. . . . She looked into his blue wet-lashed eyes and instantly forgot all she'd told herself that day.

"How've you been?" he asked softly, trailing a finger along the side cutout of the maillot.

"Oh, middlin'." She brought her arms from their bracing position behind her, around to the front again, dropping them like two stone pillars between his wandering touch and her midriff.

"I like the suit," he said appreciatively.

"I like yours," she retorted, determined to keep on an equal footing. He was like a child, wanting whatever happened to fall in his line of vision. If she hadn't windsurfed—floated—past, would they be together now? Of course not.

"Find your shoe?"

"Oh, that," she said, as if the second in a matching pair were of little significance.

"I looked for you at lunchtime. You weren't home. The door to your office was locked and you weren't lunching at the Frangipani. Should I be jealous?" He reached out and grabbed hold of a fish-trap buoy as they floated past and secured it to the sail tether; it stopped their flight downwind.

She watched a bead of saltwater glisten down the hairline of his torso and disappear into . . . well, disappear. "Don't be silly. I was one of the three hundred and fourteen revelers aboard the *Swan* for lunch. You didn't see me? The one in the G-string and tassles?"

His smile was wry. "New England puritanism runs deep, I see. String bikinis," he added, "are perfectly commonplace down here."

"I noticed," she said grimly. "But I didn't risk life and limb to discuss fashion with you. You've had another request for a charter, a Mr. and Mrs. Stevenson. They claim to have admired your boat and spoken to you in the British Virgin Islands a year or so ago. Since then, they haven't known where to reach you—who ever does?—and then they saw a photo of the *Swan*, which I happened to . . . uh . . . include in a recent ad."

He raised one eyebrow. "Accidentally, no doubt."

She ignored that. "They'd like the boat for the first week or so in February. And they'd like to bring their dog. Are you interested or not?" She would not beg this time.

"Of course I am. Sign 'em up." He actually looked pleased about it.

"Aren't you going to ask what kind of dog?" She was disappointed.

"It's not a St. Bernard, is it?"

"Scottish terrier. An *old* Scottish terrier."

"It's not infirm, is it? Or being fed intravenously?"

"They didn't say."

"I'm sure I can manage." His bantering tone dropped to a husky rasp. "I've missed you, Leda," he said abruptly. He laced both hands through her wet, dripping hair and brought his cool, salty mouth on hers in a hungry caress. Leda held tightly to the sailboard, returning the pressure of his mouth to keep herself from falling backward into the water—again.

"Oooooh! Naughty Nat-ty," came a sultry, accented voice. Leda jerked her head away from Nat's embrace in time to see

93

Juanita sail close by on her windsurfer, blowing a kiss and breaking into a wide smile. She had dimples. Needless to say.

Nat's ironic smile seemed disgustingly good-natured to Leda. She pushed him with sudden, furious force off the board, and into the water. "Don't you ever do that in public again!" she seethed.

Laughing, he grabbed her by the ankle. "Seems to me I said something similar about your dancin', love. Come on, in you go."

"No!"

"Yes!" And he pulled her, feet first, into the water after him.

Leda came up sputtering a mouthful of saltwater and rage. "Don't you touch me," she shouted, tumbling and twisting out of his arms.

"Whoa! Wait, sweetheart. God, you're as slippery as a brook trout," he shouted back, managing to grip her shoulders at last. "Look, I promise not to kiss you in public again. I promise not to touch you after I release you. And I promise I'm going to show you how to sail this thing, or die trying. As you can see," he gasped, wiping his wet hair away from his eyes, "we've drifted halfway across the harbor. You can stay tied to this buoy until dark, waiting to flag down some unsuspecting stranger for a tow. Or you can let me sail it back to the beach for you and, as part of my no-risk package, give you a free lesson in the art of proper windsurfing. Now what d'you say?"

"What am I supposed to do—walk back?"

"I'll tow you; there's enough wind. It's fun, actually."

It was. Leda lay with her stomach and chest on the back end of the board, her legs trailing in the water, lazily surveying the anchored yachts from a fish's point of view, lazily surveying Nat as he stood a foot away from her, expertly maneuvering the sailboard. He had very powerful-looking calves, not nearly so hairy as his chest, and nice knees.

"Mush. Mush," she commanded imperiously. "We're hardly moving." That woman was going twice as fast, as a matter of fact.

"Darlin', you're a pretty streamlined number; but let's face it—hydrodynamically speaking, we're in big trouble."

"Oh, yeah? How about if I rev up the horsepower?" She began kicking her legs energetically, which caused the board to wobble and Nat to be thrown off with a pretty thunderous splash of his own. Leda found herself nose-to-nose with a half-drowned, glinty-eyed mariner. "I was only trying to help," she whispered in wide-eyed innocence.

"Indeed."

The sun was low by the time Nat jumped off into the shallow water of the beach, and Leda tried her best to wriggle out of her introductory lesson. For one thing, the white sandy strip was still dotted with lounging sun-starved newcomers. For another, Juanita was still fluttering around them—Nat—like a moth around a flame. It was one thing for Leda to make a private spectacle of herself in front of Nat; it was another to do it in front of half of Bequia.

But Nat "Never-Take-No" Hardy was at his obstinate best. Standing in the shallow water up to his waist, he held the board steady for Leda. "Your mistake was elemental, love," he said. "It'll hardly be a challenge to teach you. Put your front foot farther forward on the board when you begin; that'll let you get up some speed, and it won't be so hard to balance yourself. Ready? Hop up."

It was far easier to get a foothold with Nat holding the board firmly, and in seconds Leda had the sail in position with the wind straining against it, feeling as though she was about to be shot out of a cannon.

"I'm ready, Nat," she said excitedly. "Let 'er rip!"

"Off you go!"

And off she went, accelerating at what seemed to her a breakneck speed, terrifying and exhilarating. She had gone less than a hundred yards when she heard Nat cry out behind her with a sudden howl of pain.

Leda didn't know how to get the sailboard turned around—he hadn't explained that part—and so she hurled the sail away from her, deliberately fell into the water, and bobbed up in time to see Nat staggering out onto the beach with a limping hop. Abandoning the board, she swam in seeming slow motion toward Nat, each stroke frozen in time. As soon as her feet found sandy bottom, she began wading through the water; it felt like quicksand. From out of nowhere Juanita had sailed her wind-surfer directly up and on to the beach; she was running toward Nat, who was sitting on the sand with a heart-rending grimace on his face. Two or three guests on the beach had already begun to cluster around Nat.

He'd stepped on a spiny sea urchin, and several of the long black needles were stuck in the sole of his left foot. A wave of sympathy amounting almost to nausea rolled over Leda as she dropped to her knees beside Nat.

"How deep are they?" she asked quietly.

"One is very, the others not bad," he spit out between gritted teeth.

Juanita stood above them, clenching and unclenching her fists helplessly and crying, "Oh Natty, poor, poor Natty; oh, Natty . . ." She gazed unseeing at Nat's face, then at Leda's, avoiding the protruding spines completely.

Leda stood up and gripped Juanita by her shoulders. "Juanita. Will you do something for Nat? Will you run to the bar at Coco's and bring back three limes, cut in half? Will you do that?"

Juanita nodded dumbly and scampered off like a frightened twelve year old. Leda knelt back next to Nat. For the first time she noticed that two or three spiny tips had broken off and were embedded in the same foot as well. "Will any of the intact spines come out easily?"

"This one . . . mmnf . . . will," he said, easing the shortest spine out and tossing it aside with a look of repugnance. "How did you know about limes?" he growled without looking at her, taking another one gently between his fingers and attempting to ease it out as well. "Damn!" The tip had broken off and stayed lodged in his foot.

"Wait, Nat. That last one really is deep; let's leave it until we can squeeze some lime juice into it. Can you hobble over to Coco's? If you lean on me?"

"Nothing doing."

"But Nat," she argued, a little surprised at his timidity. "There aren't any ambulances. Surely if I support your weight . . ."

"I promised, you recall, not to touch you," he said with a weak smile.

"Be serious, you idiot," she rebuked him. "Here, just . . . that's it . . . What do you think? Can you make it?" She braced her body to bear the heavy pressure of his arm against her back.

"You'll do," he said shortly. His breath came rapidly; clearly he was in more pain than he was letting on.

One or two men had offered to help them, but Nat waved them away brusquely. "Next thing you know, they'll be wantin' to carry me off in a litter." He leaned heavily into Leda, and she staggered slightly under his weight.

"Too much?" he gasped politely.

"No, just keep holding me."

"God, a golden opportunity—wasted!" he snorted.

"Shut up and keep hopping," she ordered.

They managed a few more yards by the time Juanita met them with the limes.

"Time for a break, Captain," Leda said as she eased Nat onto the sand, took the limes from Juanita, and squeezed the juice from them into the punctures.

"Juanita, stop wringing your hands," Nat said impatiently. "I'm fine."

"Why lime juice, Natty?" Juanita asked as she continued methodically to wring her hands.

"It dissolves the spines, or so they say. I've never been dumb enough to have to find out. Give Leda a hand helping me back up, would you, Rio?"

Leda looked up quickly. Rio? A little pet name between . . . friends?

With the extra support of Juanita on the other side, Nat was

97

able to hop faster, and they reached the main house at Coco's just as the last of a red ball of sun dipped serenely into the ocean.

"Now what?" Nat asked in exasperation. "The damn skiff is hanging off the *Swan*. How'm I supposed to get back?"

"Captain, if you don't mind a suggestion, there's a little room with a bed just off the kitchen in the main house; the last cook apparently was a live-in. But it's empty now, and I think the best thing would be for you to spend the night there. Even if we got the skiff for you, it'd be hard to climb aboard in the dark with one foot out of order."

"Sensibly put," he said tiredly. "Juanita, why don't you take the windsurfer back to the *Swan*. And don't worry, I'm fine. Incidentally," he said with an obvious effort, "Juanita Ryan, this is Leda Sayers. You'll forgive my earlier . . . remissness."

Leda nodded ironically and Juanita smiled a rather forlorn smile. "It is all right, then?"

"It's fine. Good night, Rio."

Juanita had barely left the old cook's room before Nat muttered, "She has a heavy date with the skipper of that trimaran anchored next to us. A pity to spoil her fun. I'm . . . exhausted."

Leda eased him onto the tiny bed, which creaked beneath his awkwardly lowered weight. For the first time she noticed, in the rather dim glare of the overhead light, how flushed his face was. His broad chest rose and fell with a shallow motion, and his forehead was dripping wet. She wished she knew more about sea urchins.

"You don't look well, Nat," she said softly, wiping away the dampness on his forehead.

"You wouldn't either if you'd just hopped for two blocks, you ninny. God, you sound like Juanita," he added petulantly. "I'd begun to give you credit with having more wits than that."

She ignored the sarcasm. "I think I should look for a doctor tonight."

"If you do, woman, I promise you won't live to pay his bill," he growled. "Look, I've heard of people who've stepped on sea

98

urchins before. It hurts for a while, and then it doesn't hurt. Simple," he said through gritted teeth, and closed eyes.

"All right then, hero; how about a slug of brandy to help you sleep?"

He opened his eyes. A slow, crooked smile tilted the mustache above his perfectly formed mouth. "I take it all back about you."

In five minutes Leda had informed Julie about her new tenant and was back in the cook's room with a largish brandy. "Drink up. I want you nodding before I experiment on you," she said, grinning.

"Sounds like I'd miss all the fun," he answered curiously. "What did you have in mind, Dr. Frankenstein?"

Leda had lit a short, fat hurricane candle. "Thomas is bartender tonight; he told me of a surefire Bahamian treatment for broken-off spines. Feeling brave, me hearty?"

"Less and less so," he said, a look of extreme caution creeping across his Roman brow.

"The idea is, I drip the heated wax over the punctures. The heat neutralizes the toxin, and the wax protects the puncture until the spines disintegrate. Are you game?"

"I would be," he said, tossing off the brandy, "if you didn't look as if you were going to enjoy it so blasted much."

"Don't take it personally. I torture all my victims before I dispatch them," she said with a sweet smile.

He stared at the empty glass in his hand. "Poisoned. I feared as much."

"Ready?" She dripped a little wax on the first puncture, and Nat jerked his foot reflexively. After that, he was able to hold himself steady.

"I didn't know you enjoyed dabbling in witchcraft," he grunted. "Yowch! Not on the toe!"

"There's a broken-off spine I didn't see before. Don't be such a baby. Okay. Now, I'll wrap this bandage around your foot, and we'll see what happens."

"Humnph. It's probably a case of biting one's finger to stop one's toothache, but the hot wax has stopped the pain a bit.

Thanks, Ms. Nightingale." His lids fluttered, the long lashes obscuring his eyes before they shut completely. "The poisoned brandy," he murmured drowsily, "is beginning to take . . . effect."

Leda lit the ancient kerosene lamp on the bedstand, pulled the light blanket over his still-damp torso, and tiptoed over to the wall switch and flipped it off. "Good night," she whispered, gazing one last time at his prostrate form. *Goodnight, my darling.*

"Leda," he said in a hazy, exhausted voice.

"Yes?"

"By now your windsurfer must be . . . halfway to Nicaragua. . . ."

Leda awoke at two in the morning from a fitful, dream-ridden sleep. How could it only be two A.M.? When she was with him, time flew at the speed of light; away from him, time stood on its head and laughed at her. She'd been under siege from a welter of emotions, and she was trying, without success, to sort them out, analyze them, put them aside, and fall asleep again.

First and foremost was her fear for Nat. When she'd looked up *sea urchins* in her medical manual, she learned that venom-related injuries were rare; the less serious, broken-spine injuries far more common. That was comforting . . . sort of. But with a tight-lipped stoic like Nat, who could be sure if he hadn't squished a sea urchin down to its venom organ, wherever that was?

And then there were the continuing waves of guilt that washed unexpectedly over her: If she hadn't tried to windsurf out to see Nat, it never would have happened. And where did Juanita fit in all of this? Juanita, who glided in and out of Leda's dreams on a blue-sailed windsurfer. How much less substantial Juanita had seemed close-up. Frightened, ravishing Rio.

And the hot-wax remedy! Surely Leda had been a little punchy at that point. This was the twentieth century, and she was practicing voodoo! She'd be cutting open a chicken next, trying to read its entrails. And the borrowed windsurfer, on its way under a starry canopy to the coast of Central America. She wondered what some fisherman would think when he came across the odd little plaything on a rocky shore one dawn. She wondered where she'd get the thousand dollars to replace it.

But first and foremost, Nat's injury. She turned on the light and looked up *sea urchins* for the eighth time in her medical manual. "If not removed, the spines may migrate into deeper tissues, causing a granulomatous nodular lesion. . . ." Why wouldn't he see a doctor? She'd never last till dawn, even if he would. Slipping a printed cotton shift over her bare, overwrought body, she padded out of the cottage half-asleep and made her way, through a night exploding with stars, to the cook's room.

Tiptoeing to just outside the open door, Leda paused and listened to Nat's rhythmic, deep breathing. He sounded perfectly normal, and she was conscious of a ridiculous surge of relief. She was becoming a silly hysteric. Ever so quietly she peeked through the doorway at his sleeping, convalescing form. He had thrown off the blanket and was still lying on his back, hardly moved from when she'd left him. If she could stand at that door with a musket across her chest, barring anyone from entering the room until Nat was completely well, she'd consider herself a happy woman.

And then she noticed that the kerosene lamp was burning a bit too brightly and sending acrid black smoke up its chimney. With infinite caution she tiptoed up to the bedstand to adjust the wick. A large hand reached around her right wrist, and an utterly seductive voice said, "Sit with me, pretty Psyche, and comfort me."

Leda sat beside him on the edge of the bed, her face aflame with self-consciousness. Nat held on to her wrist, turned it over on the bed gently, and trailed his fingers idly across the palm of her hand. "What are you doing here?" he asked in a low voice.

"Just checking for . . . for granulomatous nodules," she answered in a faltering voice.

"Find any?" His smile was sleepy, endearing, completely vulnerable. How she wanted him.

"How would I recognize one if I did?" she confessed weakly.

His encircling hand had begun to slide from her wrist, up to her elbow, and back down again, charging the hairs on her arm with stand-up electricity. So compelling had her desire become that she fell, rather than leaned, toward him, her breasts heaving and falling without restraint beneath the thin cotton of her shift.

"And is there nothing else of anatomical interest that I might show you?" he asked in the bland tones of a men's clothier.

"Certainly," she answered, in one last attempt to keep it light. "If the patient will kindly stick out his tongue I'll—" She stopped, overcome by confusion.

His deadpan response was perfectly preserved as he held her face between his hands and brought her mouth to his. "Just what the doctor ordered . . ."

She was lost. She was his, she was lost. The maddening silver sweetness of his tongue, the musky sleepiness of his breath, the teasing, stimulating prickle of his mustache all contrived to send self-control, resolve, guilt, sympathy, jealousy, and fear hurtling, like planetary debris, into the far reaches of the universe. All that was left in the core of her soul was simple, irreducible need; she needed him as drawn breath needs release.

"Leda," he whispered with a low sigh into her sleep-tangled hair, "come on top." His mouth sought hers again, and he covered it with hot, urgent kisses as he eased her full length over his. Never before had she known such bruising, painful kisses. In spite of the hurt, she pressed her mouth more fiercely to his, drew his tongue into hers, flaunted her desire, demanded his response. If she had written her need across the night sky in fire, she could not have made herself understood more plainly.

And there was no turning back. That, she understood as clearly as she understood that she was the latest in a long and possibly endless succession of women to climb into Nat Hardy's bed in the dead of night. She had taken a number, her turn had come, and she was enraptured at the imminent prospect of release, at last, from her aching need. Release; but before that, sweet, mounting ecstasy.

102

He pulled her shift up around her thighs, until the granite closeness of their contact prevented it from going any further. "Darlin'," he said in a husky voice, "no pun intended, but it's up to you. Can we—you—get this smock off?"

Leda had forgotten, in her hazy passion, that he was immobilized. She sat up, one leg striding each side of him, and pulled the cotton shift over her hips, her waist, her breasts, aware of the warm night air on her bare skin, aware of Nat's awareness of her. She eased the shift over her head from right to left, and it slid down her arm onto the floor beside the bed.

With the flat of his hands he wandered restlessly, curiously over the front of her body, cupping her breasts, sliding his hands behind her hips, bringing them forward again along the curve of her thighs. "Your body was made to be made love to, Leda," he said, a note almost of awe in his voice.

Vaguely, she was surprised. She'd always considered her body healthy, athletic, but nothing special. She was not voluptuous, yet tonight he was making her feel unbelievably seductive. "I was thinking," she said shakily, "the same about you." Her hands had been resting lightly on her ankles as he explored every inch of her skin; now she laid them, palms down, fingers outspread, on his midriff and slid them up and around his neck, bringing her mouth down on his for one more kiss. She needed one more kiss.

A low gasp of pleasure came from . . . from her? From him, from Nat. "Leda, will you take off my suit?" he asked with disarming normalcy.

"I—yes," she answered as she rather shyly hooked her fingers into the sides of his black suit and began to slide it off him. From somewhere very near, an astonished Leda Sayers was watching this new, aroused Leda Sayers with limitless interest; the old Leda Sayers had never got into the nitty-gritty of undressing a man before. For one insane second Leda closed her eyes in illogical modesty; but she opened them again, wondering, and perhaps a little awestruck herself.

Leda shifted her right leg over alongside her left so that she could peel his swimsuit the rest of the way away; and in doing so she knocked her right foot into Nat's injured one. A shudder of pain went through Nat, and she cried out with a gasp of shocked realization of what she'd done.

"Oh, no! Nat, oh, I'm so sorry!" She sank into an abyss of sympathy and mortification.

"Ah, it's nothing, really. It'll pass." He groaned, obviously and instantly unaroused. "It's nothing."

"Of course it's something. Oh, God, I don't believe this. I'd forgotten . . . I didn't mean to . . . it was . . . an accident," she whispered abjectly.

Nat sighed heavily. "Come here; lie next to me for a while and we'll just rest for a bit."

"Lie next to you? My God, I'm like a bull in a china shop. I'd probably roll over and smother you in my sleep!" she cried, filled with self-loathing. "And besides," she added dully, "it's almost dawn. The help will be in soon. I can't stay here."

"Stay here," he argued softly.

Still kneeling beside him on the bed, she reached down to the floor for her crumpled-up shift, turned it right side out, and pulled it back over her head, over her breasts, over her waist and hips, in a dejected reversal of her earlier movement. "Don't you realize how absurd this is? Drunk one time, clumsy another. I just can't seem to get it right around you, Nat. I'm beginning to think it wasn't fated to happen between us." Her voice was blank with desolation.

Nat looked at her steadily. "It won't happen between us, Leda, if you're not willing to be master of your own fate."

104

CHAPTER SIX

Leda stumbled back blindly to her cottage after that, too sick at heart to face the fact that once again she'd reached out to grab at the brass ring of ecstasy and missed. Instead she fell into a dreamless, forgetful sleep and didn't awake until she felt a warm beam of morning sun across her bare thigh. Her eyes fluttered, then shot open: nine o'clock! Slipping into a cool white cotton sun dress with flat-band straps, she ran, as fast as the heat would allow, to the tiny infirmary that operated out of Port Elizabeth.

Within half an hour Leda was adroitly balancing two crutches against two cups of coffee in the narrow hall outside the cook's room, wondering what possible tone would be the right one to strike with her hapless victim.

Nat was propped up on top of the blanket against a pillow and was staring into space, or possibly at the bandage, which looked infinitely less professional in the morning light. He was smoking a cheroot, not his first; the little shell ashtray on the bedstand was overflowing with small cigar stubs. Still bare-chested, he had changed into a pair of island "baggies," cotton boxer shorts sewn all around the middle with a band of bright print fabric. Anything cheerful seemed incongruous on Nat Hardy just now; his face was a study in gloom. His black hair was still uncombed, and tumbled over his forehead.

Leda felt as though she were peering over the edge of a smoking volcano crater when she caught, then held, his look and said, too brightly, "Hi! How's the foot?"

"Better."

She put down the coffee and stood the crutches against the wall. "These are for you."

"Thanks."

Nodding toward an empty coffee cup and the overflowing ashtray on the bedstand, she forged bravely ahead. "Looks like someone's been taking care of you."

"Right."

"Juanita?"

He stubbed out a cigar with a weary gesture. "Julie 'took care of me,'" he said ironically, "if it makes any difference." He pulled up his good leg chest-high, laced his fingers across the shin, and leaned the back of his head into the wall behind him. His long-lashed blue eyes were ridiculously distracting, and Leda wondered how a woman could look him square in the eye and stay unrattled long enough to understand anything he said. She herself was staring intently at a tiny chip in the rim of her coffee cup.

"Did I really hit you that hard?" she asked in a small voice, memorizing the color of her coffee.

His laugh was short and rather bleak. "In general, love, I'd say you did. If you can stand a stale joke, I'd say you've knocked me off my feet in more ways than one."

She looked up wonderingly. The tone in his voice sounded almost puzzled; Leda wanted to see whether his eyes were confirming the tone, or the meaning, of his words. But then, those rattling blue eyes . . .

"You seem awfully unhappy about it," she ventured.

"Naturally; my foot hurt like hell yesterday."

"I meant, you seem unhappy about the other ways I've knocked you off your feet," she said, hiding underneath the saucer of her coffee cup. Maybe it would be simpler just to hold a machete to his throat and say "Tell me how you feel about me."

It seemed almost clairvoyant, the way he picked up on her thoughts. "Leda? Don't you think it's time to talk?"

But there was something about his voice, his look, that told her she didn't want to hear what he had to say. "Leda, why won't you go to bed with me?" he asked before she had a chance to go into evasive action.

"Now that's what I call plain talking," she returned lightly. She took a slow swallow of her coffee, closing her eyes and wondering, astonished, how to reply to his mystifying question. At last she said, "Captain? That was you, wasn't it, in this bed last night? Black swimsuit? One foot filled with spines and covered with hot wax?"

"One and the same," he said with a grimace.

"No doubt there was a communications breakdown," she said, placing her cup onto the stand a little noisily and standing above him. "But from where I sat," she added dryly, "things seemed perfectly clear." Really, the man was a bona fide British eccentric.

"For pity's sake, you know what I'm talking about, Leda." He had swung his legs over the side of the bed. "Hand me those damned crutches, would you? Anything beats sitting in bed like an ailing schoolboy." He lifted his weight onto the supports and thumped two or three times adeptly around the room. "Bloody awkward things," he muttered.

Leda watched him, too distracted by his quaint movements to understand the implications of his question. He reminded her of a great broken-winged hawk, unable to comprehend his loss of grace and power.

Nat swung the crutches around and faced her. "A man wants a woman; the woman seems to want him back. But one night it takes half a dozen rum-and-citrus time bombs to put her in the proper frame of mind to accept him. The next night, a convenient accident makes the question academic. After a while, the man's got to wonder. Is it anything personally to do with him?"

Slowly, slowly it began sinking in. "You think I got drunk on purpose?"

"Well, it's not as though you tripped and fell into a vat of planter's punch," he said sardonically.

"That's ridiculous! I was hot, thirsty; I thought the drinks were mostly juice. . . ." She trailed off, aware of how inane her defense sounded.

Nat had begun to thump around the room again; and again Leda was struck by his awkward restlessness. He seemed to want nothing more than to throw off his splints and fly away out of his cage. Leda could hardly blame him; the room was so small, so barren, with only a tiny window to let in the Caribbean brightness. It didn't do Nat Hardy justice, somehow.

"Look, I'm really sorry about all this, Nat. I know you must detest being hampered. . . . What kind of accident? A *convenient* accident?" It had sunk in at last. "I kicked your foot to avoid sleeping with you, is that it?" Leda asked contemptuously. Throwing herself facedown on the bed, she let her arms dangle over the edge to the floor. "Give me a break, Captain," she said disgustedly.

But Nat, persisting in his assumed role of psychoanalyst and rejected lover, continued in an exasperatingly reasonable tone. "I don't mean you kicked me consciously, of course; but I have to tell you, Leda, that your subconscious has a mind of its own. You don't trust me as far as you can throw me, and I'd like to know why. Is it my experience? My life-style? My disgusting freedom from the need to work for a living?"

Raising herself on her elbows, Leda raked her hands through her long hair, then wove her fingers together in midair over the side of the bed. She turned her face to him; he was standing on one leg as casually as a stork, his elbows resting across the tops of his crutches. Trust Captain Hardy to bring balance and strength to the most idiotic situation.

Leda rolled back over, stood up, and with her hands on her waist, stared levelly at him. "All right, Captain. Since you ask. What I distrust is your disgusting freedom, *period*. 'Course, I'm just a small-town girl, but where I come from people still believe in telephones and mailboxes and doorbells. A person can call or write or, hell, knock on a real door if she feels like saying hi. But you? You've effectively cut yourself off from the rest of the human race. It takes a major oceanographic expedition just to drop in for a cup of tea; that's assuming a person can find your damned boat in the first place," she added indignantly.

She was working up a fine head of steam. "And, of course,

whenever you feel like it you just dog down the hatches, haul up your anchor, and leave everything—and everyone—behind." A rush of desolation washed over her, as though she'd had a premonition of things to come. "I must say, Captain, you've elevated the notion of 'hanging loose' to high art," she fumed.

"Spoken like a good little citizen," he said coolly, fixing her with one of his ironic looks. "But I think it was you who once said I was living everyone's dream. That's roughly how I feel about it myself, to tell the truth. Oh, I suppose I could do something noble—set up a fund-raising drive for some cause or other in my aft cabin—but that wouldn't really remove your objections to my life-style, would it?"

"You're a selfish bastard," she said evenly.

"Am I? In England I employ a hundred and thirty-three craftsmen who are happy to be given the chance to create a classic automobile, despite a world recession. They're proud of their skills, and the product shows it. On the other hand, if I choose to give up a good deal of my annual profits to a management team so that I can explore faraway places, what right have you to censure me?" he asked quietly.

She had none, and she knew it. But she was feeling so unavoidably a part of the routine world he'd scorned that she zeroed in on the first weak spot to appear in his argument.

"Faraway places! You were headed around the *world,* Captain. It's taken you five years to come thirty-five hundred miles. At that rate Columbus wouldn't have discovered America yet. What's holding up the show?"

Both eyebrows lifted; she'd never seen the expression on his face before, and she knew she'd cut too deep. It was too late to retract her words, and she knew his pained look would remain with her for a long time.

"Damned if I know what's holding me here. I thought it might be the cheap thrills," he said dryly, "but I guess it's really because I don't want to keep sailing the *Swan.*"

She'd hardly had time to absorb the ambiguous reference to "cheap thrills" before she caught up with the end of his sentence.

"Does that mean you're giving up the dubious pleasures of a hermit crab and plan to move back on land?" she asked, her heart lifting suddenly as though a heavy boulder had been rolled off it.

"Not at all; just that the *Swan* is too big and too fancy for cruising around the world. It's too much work; it ties me down."

She threw up her hands incredulously. "You're unreal, you know that? I could find you five zillion people who'd kill to be in your place. And here you are, griping about being too tied down! Why do you bother coming ashore at all? Look at you—hobbling around in circles like a caged bird. Why don't you fly away? Fly away to your splendid isolation? I'm surprised," she added recklessly, "that you even allow a crewmember on board. But I suppose you have your needs, like food, like water. Where do you keep her stowed? On a shelf next to the canned corned beef?"

"She fits nicely between two sheets, as a matter of fact. Which, as I think I began this conversation by saying, is more than I can attest to for you, Leda." He spoke quietly, without reproach.

She stared at him in wide-eyed ferocity. He was still leaning on his crutches, standing on one foot with irritating elegance. "I told you that last night was an accident," she repeated through clenched teeth. "This," she thundered, kicking one crutch out from under his arm, "is no accident."

He fell backward on the bed with a soft bounce, more startled than injured. "You play pretty rough, sister," he growled, leaning back on his forearms and sounding a fair amount like Humphrey Bogart. "Wanna have a pillow fight?"

"Go," she said as she turned on her heel, "to hell."

Minutes later Leda was at her desk, methodically ticking off the things she should have said, when Thelma appeared, standing behind a pair of crutches that were about even with her eyebrows.

"Cap-tain Hardy say dem be for you, Leda," the young girl said, handing over the crutches to her. "Cap-tain Hardy also say to tell you, 'Neither de borrower nor de lender be.' He say you know de man who say dat." Thelma looked impressed.

Leda smiled. "Well, not personally, Thelma. He was an American named Ben Franklin, and he meant, if you lend something to someone you might not get it back. And if you *borrow* something," she added, "you might not be able to return it."

"Such as de windsurfer?" the girl asked innocently.

"That's a very good example of what Ben Franklin meant," Leda admitted ruefully.

Thelma left and Leda found herself staring idly at the crutches. So Nat had fled to the safety and comfort of the *Swan.* She couldn't blame him. He was probably terrified of her, and with good reason. Somehow he had dug down deep into her personality and exposed a warrior-maiden. Leda had always behaved in a perfectly civil manner with all the men she'd ever known, including Jeffrey. But Nat? Since she'd arrived on Bequia she'd pushed him into the water, kicked his foot, knocked him off his crutches. And tried to slap his face, of course. Was it his fault, or hers, that she routinely resorted to violence?

His fault, she insisted to herself. He came on too strong. He was too relentless; too provoking. She slit open the top envelope of the day's stack of correspondence. *Who're you kidding,* she asked herself. It was his fault, true, but for another reason. He was the only man she'd ever met who brought out every single facet of her personality—good, bad, and in between. When Leda struck out at him, it was because she was resisting his invitation to let down all her defenses and expose herself utterly to him. And why should she, if he planned to sail away from her afterward? He certainly gave new meaning to the old phrase "love 'em and leave 'em." Nat was right; she *was* afraid to give herself to him. Not afraid, exactly, but too proud.

In the afternoon, the blond-haired owner of the abandoned windsurfer passed by Leda's office window, and she hailed him.

"Andy! I have awful news for you, but I promise I'll make everything right."

"You mean about the windsurfer? No problem. Hardy gave

111

me his. Same model, better condition; I'm not complaining." He grinned happily.

"He did what?"

"He said it was his fault that mine got lost in the first place, and he felt responsible. It sounded fair to me," Andy added judiciously.

"He did *what?*"

"Hey, Leda, don't sweat it. That guy's got money of his own. Hey, I gotta run." Andy was beginning to look very uncomfortable. Obviously he'd drawn his own conclusions about Nat and Leda, conclusions which did not jibe with the look of astonished anger on Leda's face.

It was the last straw; her pride simply could not take the kind of pummeling that Nat was giving it. She stood up, pressing the flat of her hands onto the desktop, staring down intently at nothing. He was making assumptions; making other people make assumptions. If he thought a thousand dollars was going to make her fall all soft and weepy at his feet, he was wrong, wrong, wrong. She'd borrow the money from her parents if she had to, much as she disliked the idea. She'd never be able to find an identical windsurfer for Andy, so the present arrangement would have to stand. But at least Leda would have the satisfaction of paying Nat off in cold, hard cash. How had she got herself in this mess, anyway? Involuntarily her palms clenched into fists, rose up, and came slamming down onto her desk. *Nat Hardy, that's how.*

It was the end of another crazy day in the charter trade. Things had been going chaotically haywire all week, and Leda had been kept too busy hopping from one crisis to the next to give any but an occasional thought to Nat Hardy's convalescence. He had remained aboard the *Swan,* and for once it was a case of "out of sight, out of mind."

There was simply too much going on. The big news was that Sam and Carol were splitting up. Leda had been flabbergasted when Carol ran in tearfully one morning, announcing the end of her marriage. The pressures of chartering, of almost enforced partying, and of financial obligations had overwhelmed Sam and her. Sam had responded by having a fling with another woman, and Carol had responded by taking up residence in the cook's room until the first available flight home. That was still two days away, and meanwhile Leda was trying frantically to reconcile the young couple and to rearrange their scheduled charters, just in case she had no luck.

There was also an epidemic of gear failures aboard the charter boats. A horde of gremlins had been let loose, running through the fleet and causing constant mischief. Refrigerators, generators, and engine starters all failed on cue, and torn sails and rigging failures were common. As fast as Leda made arrangements to have one boat repaired, another limped, disabled, into the harbor behind it.

Even the ship-to-shore radio that Leda had installed in her office pooped out. She was connecting the antenna wire to the back of a new radio when Julie waltzed in, holding a shimmering white dress with rhinestone spaghetti straps to her slim, tall frame.

"My dear, put all that electrical junk away. Tonight we dine in splendor aboard the *Moonraker.*"

"The huge motor yacht that just arrived? Since when?"

"Since I ran into the owner, who happens to be my dear friend Gerald Rafferty, at lunch. He asked me whether I knew a young lady to round out the party, and naturally I raved about you."

"Oh, no, Julie, really. For one thing, I don't have anything to wear on a par with that depressingly stunning dress." The *Moonraker* was the most elegant yacht she'd ever seen, in Bequia or anyplace else. She'd be as relaxed aboard the *Moonraker* as a seventh-grader at Harvard.

"Dear, you don't *need* a depressingly stunning dress; you can make it up with shapely legs and glowing skin," the older woman said bluntly. "*I* need all the help I can get. I won't listen to any arguments, Leda. I've already accepted for you, in any case." She whirled the dress around with graceful frivolity. "I hope there'll be dancing; Gerald does an inspired tango."

Leda had finished hooking up the ship-to-shore radio and flipped on channel 16. "Julie, I appreciate the trouble you've gone to, but—let's face it—I'm more comfortable barefoot on the beach than on an upper deck with the upper crust. Well," she said, sighing, "let's see if I can get this thing to work." She pressed the transmit button.

"This is Coco's Yacht Charter Service, calling any vessel in Admiralty Bay for a radio check," she intoned smoothly.

Almost immediately, an equally smooth but much lower voice came back over the air. "Coco's, this is the yacht *Swan*. I read you loud and clear. Please switch and answer on channel 68."

"Oh, *hell!*" Leda snorted, and then pressed the transmit button again. "This is Coco's, switching to 68." She had no choice. If she declined, Nat would keep calling her over the air for the rest of the day. It was just her luck that he happened to have his set turned on when she'd tried the radio check. *"Swan,* this is Coco's. Can I help you?" Her voice dripped with professional courtesy; anyone in the harbor might be listening to their conversation.

"Yes, Coco's, you can. My foot is better, and I'm bored silly. Any suggestions?" There was a lazy, suggestive smile in the voice.

"Swan, this is Coco's," she replied formally. "I suggest, Captain, that you give windsurfing a try." Miserable lout!

"Coco's, *Swan,"* he answered, mocking her formality. "I've decided to give up windsurfing; it's hazardous to my health." The smile had obviously grown to a broad grin.

"Swan, this is Coco's. In that case, perhaps you'll consider getting your boat in good running order for your next charter on Sunday." He would be gone again, this time for two whole weeks. Was this all she would have of him? A disembodied voice over public airwaves?

"Coco's—Leda—the *Swan* has had all the blasted attention it deserves. *I'm* the one who needs a little tender lovin' care just now. Can we get together this evenin'?" His voice came through a little huskily.

Instantly several new voices were heard transmitting one over the other; everyone in Bequia seemed to have been tuned in to the conversation.

"There's an offer you can't refuse, lady!" transmitted another male voice. "Take it, take it!"

"If you don't, I will," some woman responded gleefully.

Leda waited in horror for the comic ruckus to die down. Didn't anyone nowadays have any respect? Damn, bored sailors! She pressed the transmit button, aware that Julie was furiously shaking her head no while silently mouthing the word *Moonraker*.

"*Swan,* this is Coco's. We appreciate your kind offer, Captain, but we are engaged for the evening." Cripes. She sounded like Carol Burnett doing an imitation of Queen Elizabeth. "Anyway," she finished up feverishly, "this is Coco's, clearing with the yacht *Swan* and switching back to channel 16."

And then she shut off the radio. It was a little like hanging up on someone, except for the fact that fifty other men and women were involved in the proceedings. "God, this island!" she wailed. "It's a regular fishbowl!"

"Well, dear, there's no television; we all have to take our soap operas where we can find them," Julie teased good-naturedly. Her smile became more sympathetic. "Oh, never mind about us; we're all just jealous. Meet me at seven-thirty on the dinghy dock. Dress to dazzle."

CHAPTER SEVEN

Precisely at seven-thirty P.M. a white-uniformed crewmember was helping Leda and Julie into the *Moonraker*'s exquisite antique launch. Leda settled into the tufted red leather seat and rather reluctantly put a hand on a brilliantly polished brass rail to steady herself. The night was dark, but the lights from the shore shone in soft diffusion on the gleaming varnish of the bow and highlighted the shining brass guardrail that encircled the launch like a halo. The navigation lights burned bright red and green as the narrow boat cut effortlessly through the smooth water on its way to the *Moonraker,* and Leda felt that a royal carriage would have seemed a very ordinary conveyance by comparison.

The *Moonraker,* despite its great size, had been maneuvered to an attractive location near the beach. From her vantage point in the launch, Leda could appreciate the classic, majestic lines of the yacht. The deck lighting had been artfully installed to show the *Moonraker* to its greatest advantage; understated elegance shone in every square foot of its paneled varnished wood, and along every yard of its dazzling chrome rails. The launch glided to a halt at the spotless white gangway, which had been lowered down the side of the *Moonraker*'s towering hull, and the crewman jumped out ahead of the women to assist them. Very cautiously, Leda followed Julie up the teak-treaded steps, watching the yacht's lights sparkle and dance in the rhinestone straps of Julie's white dress.

Self-consciously, Leda adjusted the thin satin sash of her black gauze dress; despite Julie's lavish compliments, she felt underdressed. The striking simplicity of her black dress, with its front overlapping vee, low-cut back, and flowing skirt, now struck her as ordinary somehow. Her only consolation was that she was so deeply tanned that stockings were unnecessary, even in high heels. And her golden, shining hair was comfortably off her neck, arranged in an intricate French braid, which accented the only jewelry she really valued, a pair of antique, delicately wrought gold earrings. Still, Leda felt like a poor relation next to Julie, who had got all done up in flouncy curls and diamond bracelets and seemed to fairly shimmer and flash up the gangway steps ahead of her.

To their host, who awaited their arrival at the top of the steps, Julie gushed, "Gerald! The *Moonraker* looks divine; she's still queen of the harbor."

"There is only one queen of this harbor, Julie, and we all know who that is," he said, kissing Julie affectionately.

"Gerald Rafferty, this is Leda Sayers. What did I tell you? Isn't she absolutely gorgeous?"

Leda smiled warmly. "Mr. Rafferty, the *Moonraker* is a magnificent yacht; she has truly beautiful lines."

Rafferty was an American, fifty, silver-haired, and of medium height; his powerful build undoubtedly required special tailoring, and it showed in the cut of his navy blue blazer and white duck trousers. His smile was absolutely genuine. "Leda, my girl, do you want me to propose to you right on the spot? You certainly know the way to a man's heart."

"I promise you," Leda laughed, "that the compliment is paid without any ulterior motive."

Julie slipped an arm through Rafferty's. "He's about to offer you a tour of his lady love. I shall come along too; I haven't been aboard in, what . . . over two years now?"

"Has it been that long? You've a lot to see, then," Rafferty said with quiet enthusiasm. "The galley has been completely redone. We could try peeking in, but Lee Han is preparing dinner and would throw us out; we'll sneak in later. You've got to see it: three microwave ovens, a walk-in deep freeze, the works. Lee Han designed it all himself, of course; I just paid the bills. If he ever leaves the *Moonraker* I'll probably have to have a new freezer built; this one's only five and a half feet high."

"Lee Han leave!" Julie scoffed. "He's been with the boat forever."

"Fifteen years. We threw a surprise anniversary party for him. Did all the cooking ourselves; he still hasn't forgiven us. Let's see, we can't view the staterooms because the guests are undoubtedly dressing for dinner. What else—ah, the jade collection. I've finally had a proper cabinet made that can house it all safely. Would you care to see it?" His friendly politeness drew Leda into their little circle of intimacy.

As the three made their way below to the ship's library and its jade collection, Leda found herself speculating shamelessly about Julie Simpson and Gerald Rafferty. Obviously Julie had known him while she was still married. Just as obviously, Gerald and Julie had been intimate sometime in the past. There was a chemistry between them that added even more sparkle to Julie's high spirits tonight. Was it always so clear to bystanders when two people were in love? Were these two in love? Or was it just biological, the attraction of one brightly plumed creature for another? And where, oh, where did Leda's tumultuous feelings for Nat fit in? Love or biology?

Leda followed her host and Julie through a maze of teak-floored corridors. She wished she'd dropped a trail of crumbs behind her; without Rafferty's help she might easily become lost on the *Moonraker* forever. The library appeared at last, a softly lit, elegantly comfortable retreat. On one side was a wall of books, mostly leatherbound and unread, although one shelf held a collection of affectionately thumbed cruising stories. The opposite wall provided a paneled varnished backdrop for a collection of oil paintings and watercolors, all with nautical themes. A sea-green leather sofa complimented the green highlights of the wine-red Bukharan rug. On a low table, topped by a Greek mosaic portraying a chart of the Mediterranean, was a silver tray which held a crystal decanter and several thin-stemmed glasses.

"You'll have some sherry, of course, Julie. Leda?"

"Yes, thank you." Leda had been peering, like a child in a toy shop, into the intricately carved display case that housed the jade collection. The dark red of the cherry wood provided a rich contrast to the green and white jade artifacts within. Each was held securely from the boat's motion by a set of brass—or, for all Leda knew, gold—prongs, fastened into the shelves of the case. The curved glass front allowed unhindered viewing of the Oriental enchantment inside: sea serpents and flying fish and dolphins, and wonderfully detailed Chinese ships. Each little treasure seemed to be the focus of a separate pinpoint of light. It was a daunting display of taste and clever design, and although Leda knew nothing about jade, she knew that this collection must be priceless.

"Mr. Rafferty," she said with a queer little catch in her throat, "this is one of the most . . . most beautiful . . ." She trailed off, at a loss for words, not realizing that her face, so alive with pleasure, was saying it all.

Rafferty replied with self-conscious gruffness. "Humph. *Mr.* Rafferty. I suppose Leda calls you *Mrs.* Simpson, Julie?"

"She tried," Julie answered grimly. "She failed."

"Then dammit, Leda, call me Gerald. I feel old enough as it is, without being sirred and mistered to death. More sherry?"

"No, thank you."

"Aha! Civilization at last!" A tall, slender man with gray-streaked wavy hair stood in the doorway, both hands plunged elegantly into the pockets of his gray flannel trousers. "Evening, Gerald. I've been knocking around this great ghost of a ship for the last ten minutes, looking for signs of life. All I found was a chef, and *he* brandished a cleaver at me," the visitor said in a pleasant baritone. He sauntered up to them, smiling and expectant.

Rafferty did the introductions—rather coolly, Leda thought. Their visitor was Charles Jansen, a distant cousin of Rafferty's and a guest aboard the *Moonraker* for the next week. He'd flown in to Martinique from New York the day before, which explained his wintry whiteness; and he'd recently been widowed, which explained the enthusiasm with which he attached himself to Leda.

"Cousin," Charles said smoothly, "the beautiful Leda is mine, at least during dinner. I refuse to sit next to that old what's-her-name again tonight. My God; she's *my* age. We have nothing in common."

As Charles bantered with his host, he looked at Leda too warmly, stood next to her too closely, and packed far, far too much hopefulness into his voice. She disliked him, but she had no idea whether it would be bad form to show it. So she remained stiffly in place, a frozen smile on her face.

Unfortunately her host, probably wishing to avoid any awkwardness, seemed prepared to throw Leda to the wolf. "I suppose that can be arranged," he said distantly. "In the meantime, let's join the other guests, shall we?"

Leda felt uncomfortably like a Roman slave at market. The prospects for a pleasant, entertaining evening seemed suddenly dim. As for the offer she'd turned down earlier that day, she didn't want to even think of it. She and Charles fell in behind the other couple and emerged eventually on the afterdeck, where cocktails and elaborate trays of hors d'oeuvres were being served to half a dozen guests by yet two more uniformed crewmen.

The guests were clustered in a smallish knot, surrounded by a vast semicircle of sofas covered in pale blue and green cotton duck. Leda wondered whether the guests were huddled together in self-defense, or whether they were afraid to sit down on the pristine upholstery. Two of the party seemed friendly, but two or three others seemed aloof. One guest, a woman, was too drunk to be either friendly or aloof. Her name was Brenda, she wore a yellow silk jump suit, and she found everything everyone said to be too funny for words. At one point Brenda flung out her arms by way of emphasis, completely forgetting that she held a martini in her right hand. The liquid, and the olive, went flying across the beautiful fabric that no one would sit on.

"Oh, how stupid of me! But then, at least it wasn't red wine," she giggled, and asked for another martini. A steward quietly mopped up the sofa.

Charles steered Leda by the elbow to a quiet corner of the afterdeck. "Brenda's really something, isn't she? Incredibly uninhibited," he said laughingly. "Why are you looking so glum, my dear?"

"My shoes hurt, and I'm afraid to sit on the sofa," Leda answered lightly. But she was actually wondering whether she had seemed so ridiculous the other night at the Sunny Caribee when she had been in an "incredibly uninhibited" state of her own.

"If your shoes hurt, take them off. You're too tall in them, anyway; I like my women to be more manageably sized," Charles laughed, smoothing a graying temple with a well-manicured hand. "Now take Brenda, for example . . ." he began.

"Yes," she answered curtly, "why don't you?" A whole evening of this bore? She'd never last. Leda turned away from him and stared out at the twinkling lights of the harbor. It was the most unromantic situation she'd ever been in.

Charles was giving her an appraising look. "Funny. With that hairdo, that dress—you didn't look like a fighter. A little slow to warm up, maybe; but definitely not the feisty type."

"I'm sure you'll forgive me," she said coldly, "if I don't, as they say, deign to reply." Why was everyone leaving her alone with him? Where was Julie? Where was Gerald?

Scanning the little knot of guests in desperation, Leda decided to force herself on the fierce-looking Mrs. Davis, whom Charles had been so anxious to avoid; any port in a storm. "Are you staying aboard the *Moonraker* for a while, Mrs. Davis?" Leda asked politely.

Mrs. Davis, who still retained hints of the fair-haired beauty she must have been, gave Leda an icy little smile. "I'm staying a week—the same as Charles Jansen, whom I see you've left in the lurch. Well, you're certainly safe with me; he won't come within ten feet of you now," she said with blunt shrewdness.

"Oh no, he . . ." Leda stammered unhappily. Was she

121

doomed to spend the evening at a loss for words? She'd got in way over her head when she stepped aboard the *Moonraker*. The pulsing intrigue was beyond her; everyone seemed to want someone who wanted someone else. All Leda had wanted was a close-up look at a beautiful boat and—she admitted—a close-up look at how the other half lived. Well, now she knew. They had battalions of servants, and they didn't pull their punches. Leda accepted a shrimp canapé from a crewman moving discreetly among the guests and decided that cheese and crackers in the Red Cottage beat canapés on the *Moonraker* by a country mile.

Quietly excusing herself, Leda began to saunter toward the couple she had originally dubbed "friendly." The sound of Rafferty's voice boomed out enthusiastically from the starboard deck, and she looked up curiously. At the same time, Charles sidled up to her and slipped an arm around her waist.

Rafferty was calling over his shoulder, "Hardy, you son of a bitch! How the devil *have* you been?"

Leda swung around out of Charles's grasp and said angrily, "Don't."

Their host stood before them, one hand on Nat's shoulder. "Everyone—I'd like you to meet Nathan Hardy, the best damned poker player in the Caribbean. Which reminds me," Rafferty said to Nat, "I want a game later tonight, or I'll see to it that you never leave the *Moonraker* alive."

"I'm sure your guests will have other amusements lined up," Nat said dryly, looking at Leda, then past her to Charles.

As Rafferty hurried through the introductions, Leda edged even farther away from Charles, thunderstruck by the coincidence: Nat was a dinner guest on the *Moonraker!* And, she realized with helpless longing, he was easily the handsomest dinner guest on the *Moonraker* as well. She'd never seen Nat in standard yachting dress—blue blazer and white flannels—before. His clothes were no more impeccably tailored than anyone else's; but he alone carried them completely without pretension. Next to him every other male guest looked shorter, paler, duller, less important.

Brenda took to him immediately. "Ooh, a beard. Beards are

so nautical," she said breathlessly. She seemed suddenly much more sober.

Julie had come up to Leda from somewhere. "How nice. Natty is coming to dinner, too. Leda, do you want to powder your nose? You look a bit flushed. The ladies' room is down that little aisle and to the left."

"No, Julie, I'm fine. What in God's name do you suppose Nat's doing here?" Leda whispered.

"You know how small the yachting community is. Now that I think of it, *I* brought Nat as my guest to a party on the *Moonraker* the last time it was in Bequia. It seems to me I left without him and . . . yes, he stayed behind for an all-night card game. He walked off with all of Gerald's money, which wasn't very polite."

The two women watched in growing amazement as Brenda lifted one arm around Nat's neck, said something in a low giggle, polished off the last of her martini, and tossed the crystal glass over the rail and into the harbor.

"Can you beat that?" Leda whispered, a little awestruck. "Who *is* she?"

"The girl friend of that mortified-looking young man, who is —or was—an up-and-coming young executive in Gerald's construction company. Will you look at the expression on Nat's face?" Julie laughed. "I think he's afraid Brenda's going to unzip her jump suit. He's blushing like a schoolboy."

He did in fact look uncomfortable, which lightened Leda's spirits immeasurably.

A white-jacketed steward walked up to Gerald, who had been carrying on a quietly intense conversation with Brenda's young man. Gerald turned to his guests. "Shall we go in to dinner?" he asked, offering Julie his arm. Nat did the same for the blue-gowned Mrs. Davis, who glared daggers at Charles. Charles slithered happily back to Leda's side. Brenda was assigned to the aloof husband; her boyfriend, to the aloof wife. Amazingly, the friendly couple got to go in together. Perhaps, Leda thought, there was some justice in this world after all.

The formal dining cabin was sumptuously appointed in intricately paneled rosewood and mahogany. At one end, a tall recessed cabinet displayed an extravagant collection of Waterford crystal behind leaded-glass panes. At the opposite end, a marble-topped buffet with inlaid drawer fronts, highlighted in gold leaf, held an assortment of covered silver dishes. An exquisite brass and crystal chandelier, scaled to yacht proportions, hung over the damask-covered dining table, which itself was nearly lost under an elaborate setting of china edged in delft and gold, and a bewildering array of crystal stemware.

"Twelve is too many to seat at this table," Charles muttered peevishly between spoons of his bouillabaisse.

"I expect some of us were last-minute decisions," Leda said, glancing across the table at Nat, who was arguing enthusiastically with his host over the proper way to cook lobsters. "I know I was." She slipped off her shoes and rubbed her aching feet with criminal abandon into the thick wool of the ivory-and-blue Chinese rug; clearly her feet had changed shape after nearly a month of wearing sandals.

"Just plunge the little devils into boiling water," Rafferty was insisting, "and that's that."

"Ah, but as in everything else, there's a fashion in these things," Nat argued. "The new, humane way to cook lobster is to put them in a pan of lukewarm water and slowly bring it to a boil. The lobsters drift gently off into unconsciousness—and the meat, theoretically, stays more tender. What do you think, Miss Sayers," Nat said, turning to Leda with innocent friendliness. "If you wanted to dispatch a creature, would you do it suddenly and cruelly, or slowly and gently?" His blue eyes danced with innuendo.

"You sound like someone out of an Agatha Christie mystery," she said with a polite smile. "I shouldn't think the lobster would be very happy, either way." Wretch! He was teasing her about the way she'd treated him after his injury.

"I propose a toast," Brenda said suddenly, pushing her chair back, standing, and raising her wineglass aloft, almost without spilling any. "To all the dear little lobsters who've given their lives so that *we* could have bouillabaisse. Hip, hip . . ."

"Sit *down,*" growled her escort, furious with embarrassment.

Julie interrupted in her pleasant voice. "Gerald, are you going to let me rummage through all your old records later? I was telling Leda that you're an inspiration on the dance floor."

"As a matter of fact, Julie," Rafferty answered quickly, "I've something better planned. But don't ask me any more questions; it's a surprise."

"If we have to play charades again tonight, I swear I'll swim ashore," Charles whispered to Leda all too loudly.

She wanted to cover her head with her napkin and slide quietly under the table. Mercifully, several people began to speak, which eased her immediate embarrassment. But Leda resolved to avoid Charles in every way possible after that, and fell into conversation with the friendly couple, who were perfectly courteous and charming. They were very curious about Leda's job and asked penetrating, intelligent questions.

"How can you possibly keep all those yacht captains in line, Leda?" Christine asked, her gray eyes sparkling with curiosity.

Somehow Nat picked up the question from his end of the table. "She kicks 'em and shoves 'em in line, that's how," he answered cheerfully. "And when all else fails," he added, dabbing the tips of his mustache with his napkin, "she drags out her cat-o'-nine tails."

"Captain Hardy makes me sound meaner than I am, Christine. I've never used a 'cat' on him," Leda said sweetly.

"All I can say to that," Nat retorted, "is I hope the wench never gets command of her own ship."

"That's silly, of course," Leda answered with a bright smile. "I get along very well with others."

"Oh, she can give orders like a rear admiral. Can't follow 'em worth a damn, though," Nat added amiably as he sliced into his leg of lamb.

Leda glanced at Julie to see if there was any moral support coming from that corner. Nope. Julie was content to watch the duel with an amused half-smile. So, for that matter, was everyone else; even Brenda had quieted down. Leda was on her own.

Suddenly self-conscious, she faltered, "I don't see why you say that."

"That you can't follow orders? It's funny that this topic should come up, actually; because I was wondering just a few hours ago what the single most valuable asset of a crewman is, and I decided that it's the ability to follow orders. Now, Juanita, for all her aggravating faults, has that ability. Juanita," he explained to the company, "is my crew. She's as faithless as the female species allows; but I can trust her completely to follow an order. I know she's not going to argue, or go off and do it her own way, or ignore me altogether. And then I wondered how *you* would do in Juanita's place," he continued, raising a glass of Burgundy to his lips and looking Leda directly in the eye, "and I realized that the charter would probably be doomed."

"Doomed!" Laughter rippled around the table as Leda choked back her indignation.

"Certainly. Your damned arrogance would get in your way every time," he said evenly.

The barb was perfectly aimed. After an evening spent with the insufferable Charles, Brenda, and Mrs. Davis, Leda wished more than ever to be thought of as gracious and obliging—like Julie and Christine and Gerald. Her fervent desire to be dissociated from the former group made her insist recklessly, "Of course I could take orders from you—in a professional situation," she added hurriedly.

"Ha!" It was Charles. "I wouldn't bet on it," he said, motioning to the steward for more wine.

"Well, I would." Julie had jumped into the fray at last. "I'm bored silly with this idea that modern women can't take orders. It's simpleminded and insulting. Leda is a professional and would be equally good at giving *and* taking orders," she said spiritedly.

Nat's face broke into a condescending grin of disbelief. "Oh? How much would you care to bet that Leda couldn't last through a week's charter on the *Swan?*"

126

"How would we prove that, either way?" Julie asked logically.

"Simple," Nat replied. "Juanita's just told me that Sunday's charter will be her last aboard the *Swan*. I'd only planned to take one more charter after that, anyway—the couple with the aging terrier. But now I'll have to cancel, unless I can find someone to fill in for Juanita. I've checked around the harbor; there's no one available. You can spare Leda, I'm sure, for a cause so worthy."

"Well, yes," Julie answered confusedly, "I suppose I can. . . ."

"Hold it. Hold it." Leda had been listening with mounting disbelief. Juanita, leaving? Leda, replacing? Was anyone going to ask *her* opinion on the matter? "I really can't just walk out on my job for a week, even for Nat Hardy," she told him coolly.

"Oh, yes, you can," Julie contradicted her. "I can handle the office for a week; I did before, you know," she added with reproach in her voice.

"I knew it," Charles said smugly. "She's backing out. All talk."

Even Gerald Rafferty joined in the fun. "Is it too late to put a little wager on the outcome?"

Leda, feeling overtaken by events, looked around the table. She saw amusement, condescension, earnestness—and Nat's deeply interested clear-eyed gaze.

"Captain?" she said.

"Yes?"

"You're on."

And those were the last words she spoke to him until everyone reassembled on the upper deck, where Gerald had wisely chosen to have coffee and dessert served. High above the water, cool and comfortable and deliciously tempted by chocolate mousse and excellent coffee, Leda had begun, despite herself, to yield to a sense of well-being. It must be nice, she thought dreamily, to be able to have the very best of everything: the best wines, the best food, the best art, the best music. For there was music; that was Gerald's surprise. Not a symphony orchestra, perhaps, but a full twelve-man steel-drum band—one player, Leda calculated lazily, for every person in the dinner party. The band had been playing easy, pleasant music while the guests indulged in the tempting array of desserts and liqueurs.

But then the tempo had begun to change, and the stepped-up, driving beat lured some of the guests onto the teak-planked dance area. Brenda was first, dragging her downtrodden boyfriend behind her. Julie and Gerald followed and were having fun, and so were Christine and her husband. The aloof couple sat stuffily to one side in the shadows, watching and uninvolved. Poor Nat was cornered by Mrs. Davis, who was going on in an endless, animated monologue. That left Charles, hovering like a hummingbird around Leda, trying to coax her to dance.

"I really don't feel like dancing," she told him coldly for the third time. She'd rather dance with Count Dracula, if the truth were known.

And then an unlikely ally came to Leda's rescue. Brenda, pouting prettily, came up to Charles. "I've been abandoned, and I've just *got* to dance. Charley, darling, dance with me. Dance with me all night long."

Charles, a mere human, switched loyalties instantly and trotted onto the dance floor behind Brenda, and Leda was left blissfully alone to enjoy the music, the mousse, and the starry night. She decided to take a turn around the deck, and before long found herself all the way forward, standing in the dark at the bow and imagining. Imagining that she was crossing the Mediterranean, crossing the Atlantic, the Caribbean, the South Pacific, the Coral Sea. Only not in a huge motor yacht, but in a smaller boat, a sailboat. And not with a dozen crew in attendance, but with only one other. . . .

The faint, acrid smell of a lit cheroot sent erotic associations tingling through Leda's subconscious, and she turned around suddenly to see Nat in the shadows behind her, one arm folded across his chest, the other resting on the folded arm, holding a smoking cigarillo.

"I've been quiet as a dormouse," he said, smiling. "How did you know I was here?"

"I smelled your . . ." She fluttered a finger toward his cigar.

"But I was downwind of you," he protested, approaching her.

She shrugged. She'd been tracking his presence automatically all evening—exactly as if he'd been a blip on some internal radar screen in her head. It was nothing he needed to know.

"I'd like to thank you for letting yourself be goaded into taking the charter with me," he said softly. "I needed you." He flipped the cheroot stub over the rail and together they watched the fiery arc of its path end abruptly in the black water.

"I agreed to go because I was shocked that Juanita could just walk out on you at the height of the season; I wanted to make it up to you. After all, you have such a rotten view of women in this business, anyway. I guess I can't stand it anymore when you treat me as if I were just another nitwit."

"You *are* a nitwit," he interrupted impatiently, "if that's what you think. Ah, I get it; you're fishing for compliments. All right. All right. I can pay a compliment when it's deserved. You're *not* a nitwit."

"Gee, thanks."

"In fact, you're the most intelligent, accomplished woman I've run into in the charter business. But I still say you can't—won't—follow an order when you're actually aboard a boat. You'll take it too personally. You'll never be able to forget that we're male and female instead of simply captain and crew."

"In that case," she said loftily, "maybe you should hire Carol. Did you know that Carol and Sam are separated? It would probably do Carol some good to get away from Bequia for a bit."

"How crushingly professional of you, darlin'." He had leaned back, elbows on the rail, and was looking desperately appealing. "Wouldn't you be just a little jealous?" he asked wistfully.

"A little," Leda admitted softly. She leaned her forearms on the rail next to him, instinctively closing with him.

"You look very, very beautiful tonight, Leda," Nat murmured, reaching out his hand to trace the coiled intricacy of her

French braid. "It's almost sinful the way you outshine other women."

"Golly, it's a good thing I didn't wear my diamond tiara," she quipped, her voice faint with pleasure. And then: "Even Brenda?"

"Brenda?!" he repeated. "How can you even ask? She looks like a banana."

Leda laughed. "That banana peel she's wearing probably cost a thousand dollars. Charles seemed impressed with her," she added, feeling a bit feline.

"Charles would've gone after anything that moved," Nat said flatly. "Besides, I bet Brenda fifty bucks that she couldn't unfasten him from you."

Leda caught her breath sharply. Did he always trail after her with his wallet open? "Thanks for the compliment," she said ironically. "Too bad about your fifty bucks, though; why didn't you just challenge him to a duel?"

"This was more insulting," Nat answered contentedly.

"Speaking of payoffs and insults," she followed up, suddenly roused into a renewed sense of righteousness, "thanks *awfully* for donating one of your windsurfers to Andy; I should be able to pay you back on Monday."

He acknowledged the dry tone of her voice with an exasperated shrug. "I wish you wouldn't, Leda. I had two; I only need one."

"But that's not the point!" she sputtered, turning to face him.

"No, the *point,* as I've said all along, is that damned pride of yours. It's always there, like a brick wall between us." He was standing now, facing her, palms outspread in the air between them, pushing against an invisible wall. "Damn wall," he growled. "I'm tired of it. It's coming down. Now. Brick by brick."

With his right hand he lifted an imaginary brick and threw it over his shoulder, into the water. Then another, with his left hand. Then with both hands, faster and faster, he lifted and tossed more and more bricks, moving down the whimsical wall between them. Completely bemused, Leda watched the top of his head as he lowered himself to a resting position on the back of his calves.

"Hey, lady." He grinned, looking up at her, his face dancing with expectation.

"Yeah?" she answered sternly, gazing down and biting the inside of her lip to keep the smile from spilling out.

"The bottom bricks are cemented to the deck." He stood up. "Now what?"

"Dear me," she said primly, "then there's only one thing to do." Lifting her skirt with the thumb and middle finger of each hand, Leda stepped gingerly over the imaginary bricks, to within half a breath of Nat's lips. "How's that?"

"That . . . is perfect."

Cupping Leda's smiling face with his hands, he brought his mouth down on hers in a kiss of such infinite tenderness that illogical tears sprang to the corners of her eyes. In the hazy sweetness of her response, she thought that the welling in her eyes must be from the overflowing of her heart with love for him . . . because she did love him. She had tried not to, and she had failed; it was the sweetest loss she had ever suffered.

There were more reasons for loving him than she could possibly count; but just now there was really only one: He had let her decide to come to him on her own. When at last he released her lips from his, she whispered, "Thank you, Captain."

"You're welcome. For what?" he added, trailing his lips back and forth in the curve of her neck and shoulder.

"For . . . for letting me step across the bottom bricks myself."

He wrapped his arms around her and gave her a breathtaking squeeze. "You know, for a moment there I hadn't the foggiest idea what you'd do. You didn't hear my heart thumping through my chest?"

She held his face between her hands and drank in the wonder of it. "How could I? My ears were pounding from the sound of my own."

Again he held her, squeezed her; so hard that she laughed

with a kind of joyful pain, or painful joy, she didn't know which.

"Leda, my God, I was dying by degrees tonight. All through dinner, I just wanted to . . . to make contact, to touch you. I knew that you had your shoes off . . ."

"You did?"

". . . because my napkin slipped to the floor, and I saw your bare feet when I bent down for it. And—I swear—it was only through an act of heroism that I didn't grab your bare ankles, pull you under the table, and make love to you then and there."

He kissed her more quickly, hungrily, on her eyelids, her cheeks, her ears, her mouth, his voice becoming husky with longing. His hands had slipped inside the low-cut back of her dress, and her breath came more quickly under his familiar, slightly callused, totally arousing touch.

Leda was remembering, now, some more reasons why she loved him, as her tongue fluttered briefly, then fell, under the teasing, then vanquishing movements of his own. Her hands—she had no idea where her hands were; they seemed to have minds of their own, but she thought hazily that perhaps they were undoing the belt of his white flannels. Her breath came in low, quick gasps, in restless counterpoint to Nat's ragged, husky breathing.

"Nat, this is insane," she panted. "There must be somewhere else. . . ."

"Yoo hoo! Everybody! Here they are; I've found them!"

CHAPTER EIGHT

Possibly there were worse things than being discovered on the bow of a fancy yacht in the arms of your lover-to-be, mindlessly trying to unbuckle the belt of his trousers. Possibly, but Leda thought not. Neither, apparently, did Mrs. Davis, the stiff-lipped matron who succeeded in hunting them down. The party had got into full swing and, since the disappearance of Brenda's boyfriend, male partners were in short supply; so Nat was drafted into service with Mrs. Davis. Leda danced alternately and obliviously with the other men in the dinner party. When she stepped on someone's toes she forgot to apologize; when someone stepped on hers, she hardly felt it. Her mind and heart were wrapped up completely in thoughts of the man she loved.

The man she loved! How easy, suddenly, to think of Nat that way. After all her kicking and screaming, he had proved ultimately irresistible, anyway. It was far easier, Leda thought dreamily, to admit to herself that she loved him than to insist she didn't. So when Nat and Mrs. Davis whirled close to Leda and her latest partner, and Nat's eyes sought hers in a look of devilish complicity, she sent him back a look of hunger, yes; but also of joy and love. *I want you, Nat Hardy, and I'm so damned happy about it, because I love you.*

Never having been in love—like this—before, Leda was a little indefinite about its advantages. The thought flitted through her mind that one person being in love was a little like one hand clapping—not terribly satisfying in the long run. But these were abstract, philosophical considerations, to be worked out some other time.

For now the concrete, the real, the inevitable, was dancing

within five feet of her, torturing her with his tantalizing nearness. For the rest of the evening she lived for the occasional split second of contact: the time the blue linen of his blazer brushed her bare shoulder; the time he touched her fingers lightly in handing her a glass of wine.

When the band announced its last number, a slow, haunting waltz, Leda found herself in his arms at last.

"Why haven't you danced with me before this?" she whispered, more curious than offended. The night had not yet begun for them both; that was understood.

"I'm saving," he murmured, holding her at arm's length with old-fashioned correctness.

"Then why dance with me now?" she countered logically.

"Ah, well, nobody's perfect," he admitted, nodding politely to the rest of the dancers as he waltzed Leda around the dance area with well-schooled grace.

Somehow the party drew to an end. The small talk wound down, the guests began dispersing, the card game was deferred, and those who needed a ride were taxied ashore. Somehow— Leda never knew quite how—she and Nat drifted aimlessly home, laughing wickedly over Brenda the Banana, crusty Mrs. Davis, and poor cousin Charles; interspersing their teasing with quick, stolen kisses, and once or twice with drawn-out, lingering ones; murmuring nonsense, their eyes shining with fascinated delight in one another. Leda knew, during that endearing drift back to the Red Cottage, that she loved Nat with frightening intensity.

And yet, after they kicked off their shoes inside, Leda saw misgiving in his eyes, and her confidence plummeted. Nat threw his blazer over the back of the wicker armchair and leaned back against the little kitchen sink, arms crossed, giving her a searching look.

"Is something wrong?" she asked quietly.

"Wrong? Nothing's wrong . . . except for this feeling I have that I'm about to rob a kid of her candy bar. Leda, I have a confession to make. Hell, I don't make confessions; this is ridiculous." He turned away from her, palms outspread on the counter, and stared down at the faucet. "Leda, this in no way affects my feeling for you, but you have this thing about trust, and I just feel you should know that the Stevensons, the ones with the terrier—they're planning to buy the *Swan* if the charter goes well." He turned to face her. "They got in touch with me yesterday."

She looked at him in dismay, a sinking feeling in her stomach. "To *buy* it! But . . . but where will *you* live?"

His shoulders lifted eloquently. "I'll live wherever men live when they're between boats. On a desert island, in somebody's bathtub, a London hotel. Under your bed, if you'll let me. I've hardly had time to think about it."

"But *why?*"

". . . sell the *Swan?* It really is too much work. It's a very complicated machine, loaded with toys and gadgets for the idle rich. I don't need it, and I don't want it. I don't want to charter anymore. I want the independence a boat brings, not the complications."

"But a person can't party *all* the time," she couldn't resist saying, still reeling from his announcement.

"As a matter of fact, I'm not at all keen on parties. The only reason I was aboard the *Moonraker* tonight was because I found out you'd be there," he said simply.

He didn't like parties. Was he serious? She looked away from the warmth in his eyes. "What about that . . . that orgy on the *Swan* the day I tried to windsurf out to you?" Out it came, before she'd had a chance to think.

"The orgy. Let's see, when did I have my last orgy?" he ruminated, staring up at the ceiling and rubbing his bearded chin between his thumb and forefinger. "Yes, yes, I remember. Juanita had a dozen of her friends over for lunch on deck, and I was down below, up to my elbows in crankcase oil from an engine leak. Do I have the right orgy?" He grinned innocently.

"That's the one, I guess." Her voice sounded very small and stupid to her.

"Leda," he said with a wry, exasperated smile, "you have the most incredibly glorified ideas about life aboard a charter boat.

135

The *Swan* is just a business, about as glamorous as owning and operating a restaurant. In a couple of weeks, you'll be able to see for yourself."

A whole week with him aboard the *Swan;* it was too good to be true. And yet, could she bear to be that close, become that much more used to him, knowing it might be the last week he'd be in Bequia? Could she bear *not* to? Any more than she could bear not to be close to him tonight?

He had been so careful not to touch her, not to influence her unduly with his nearness, his scent, his lips. But he'd forgotten to close his eyes, and his look caressed and beseeched, more than ten thousand words could have done. Still, he'd played fair. He'd made no empty promises. Her heart was the first to acknowledge it: She trusted him.

"I'm glad you told me, Nat," she said softly. "It lets me consider . . . you know . . . things, as an adult. *So,* can I get you a drink?" she asked, staring at one of the tiny red anchors on his dark-blue tie.

"I don't think so, love," he smiled, raising his hands to her hair, carefully probing her braid for hairpins, and beginning to remove them, one by one.

"I don't have . . . maybe some Ritz crackers?" she whispered, rapidly becoming spellbound by his closeness, his scent, his gentle touch.

"Leda," he said softly, fanning the loosened plaits of her braid into a shimmering freefall over her shoulders, "this time it's right."

"Does that mean," she murmured in a state of near-hypnosis, "that you don't want me to be the perfect hostess?"

He had wrapped her hair around his fists and was pulling her slowly toward him. "I'd so much rather you were the perfect mistress," he answered, bringing his mouth tentatively over hers.

Her arms slid around his back, tracing the shifting up-and-down line of muscles as he moved his own arms from her hair, down the curve of her neck and along the cut of the back of her dress. But something . . . something was wrong. It was no use; the word *mistress* kept floating maddeningly in and out of her consciousness. She pulled back, bringing her hands to rest on his chest.

"Nat, I don't want to be anybody's mistress," she said unhappily, knowing perfectly well that he had meant the word only in a general sense.

"Oh, my; you mean you're *not* the owner of a large estate?" he teased, tilting her chin up so that she could meet his eyes. "All right then, my lady. Will you be my . . . love? Please, be my love?" His voice was low with heart-melting warmth; he brought his mouth back over hers, inviting her to join him on a tour of the universe.

Leda accepted the invitation; how could she not? A low sigh of abandonment caught in her throat as she brought her arms up around his neck, seeking the silvery taste that had made her so addicted to his kiss. And as in the case of the addict, the resulting euphoria was not enough; Leda wanted to go higher, and then higher.

"Ah, Nat, I've wanted you so, I really have," she whispered as she curved her neck to one side, exposing it to the hot-lava flow of his kisses.

"I know, sweet," he murmured, nuzzling her throat. "What I don't know is how I've managed to wait this long." He slipped the black fabric of her dress off her shoulders, exposing the untanned semicircle of her breasts, then reconsidered and pulled the dress back up.

"That bed," he laughed shakily, "is fifteen feet away, but it may as well be fifteen miles." He took her by the hand and gave her an endearingly weak grin. "What d'you say? Want to make a dash for it?"

Leda smiled and nodded, a little wobbly herself, and in an instant, he had propelled her to the bed, where they collapsed on the soft mattress, a tangle of arms and legs.

"Thank God that's over," he said, his long-lashed blue eyes very, very close to her translucent green ones. "Well, my lady," he added in a huskier voice, "are you ready for the next level?"

"That depends," she said, reaching up her hand to brush

137

away a black curl that had tumbled over his forehead, "on the qualifying exam. What do I have to do, more chin-ups?"

"Nope. You're strong."

"Tongue twisters?"

"Hopeless. We won't even try."

"What then?" She was smiling warmly now, completely relaxed, waiting with pleasurable anticipation.

"You could start by taking off my tie," he said. He was propped up on one elbow, the side of his face resting on his palm, the index finger of his other hand tracing the line of her collarbone and drawing a little path down to the cleft of her breasts.

"That's easy." She smiled, loosening the knot of his tie and pulling away the short end. She was a child opening her present slowly, by first untying the bow. The silk tie went on the floor. "Now what?" she whispered.

"Well, as near as I can calculate, I'm wearing six removable items—that's counting pants and belt as one, but figuring socks separately. *You,* brazen little seductress, are only wearing two."

"But you've already removed half a dozen hairpins!" she protested with sly innocence.

He jumped up suddenly and stood next to the bed. "Lady, tell you what I'm gonna do," he said in a comic American accent. "I'm going to remove, free of charge, one shirt, one combination of white pants and brass-buckled belt, and *two* socks." And then he was standing, in T-shirt and knit shorts, hands on his hips, letting his gaze wander over her expectant reclining form. "Now we're even," he said quietly.

Leda had seen him wearing far less, of course, but there was something so promisingly imminent about underwear. A strange little tightness gathered under her breastbone and she said softly, "It's my serve, then." Sitting up, she reached behind and unzipped the short zipper at the back of her dress.

Nat sat back down next to her, hooking his fingers under her dress at the shoulders and sliding it down to her elbows, past the tanned skin, the white skin, past the swelling tips of her breasts. "Buried treasure," he said, his voice vibrating with passion and sending a corresponding waver through Leda.

He was so absurdly adept at putting her at ease. He made it perfectly natural for Leda to reach over, to murmur "My turn, Captain"; to slip his T-shirt over his head, and to drop it on the mounting pile of hopelessly crumpled clothing.

Lacing his hands through her hair, he brought his lips slowly to hers, easing her onto her back in one fluid motion. Once again she floated high, high up, drugged into euphoria from his kiss. "Be careful of this bed," she smiled dreamily. "Sometimes, like now, it can float."

"Perfect; you can practice for our charter," he said, trailing a line of kisses from her mouth, down and across her neck, and then lower to her breasts, which rose and fell with greater and greater longing under his kisses. She arched her back, lifting her breasts closer to him. Her hands traced the hard muscles of his arms and trailed across his broad back; she was vaguely aware that Nat Hardy was really the first man she'd ever known who possessed the vaunted "sailor's physique."

His warm, wet tongue continued to play over the aching tips of her nipples as he cupped one breast, then the other, in his hand, kneading the soft flesh, reducing Leda to a state of liquefied metal. And then his tongue charted a new course, quivering down the line of soft golden fuzz between her breasts and navel, curiously, leisurely. . . . When he reached the cloth of her folded-down dress he slipped his hands into the waistline and drew the black fabric down, down, Leda raising her hips to ease its removal. Most of the dress slid over the side of the bed, but part lay caught around her ankle as Nat retraced with his tongue the trail up, up her leg, along the inside of her thigh.

Leda lay still, the top of her left forearm resting across her brow, totally a slave to sensation. It occurred to her, mistily, that she should be more bold, more forceful as a love-mate; but just this once, if she could just lie back and absorb the pleasure he had to offer. . . .

She felt his warm breath on her cheek; shivered under the loving touch of his tongue over her ear; listened in light-headed rapture as he murmured her name, murmured endearments. His fingers slid below her midriff and wandered restlessly over her silken panties, the last insubstantial barrier to his conjurer's touch. And then those, too, were gone, and before long her hips began to lift slightly and fall in an instinctive appeal for satisfaction.

All the responsive joy she had been feeling was no longer enough; she wanted, desperately, to give him as much pleasure as he was giving her. "I've been having all the fun, Captain," she said huskily. "Is that fair?"

The crumpled heap became one last garment higher and her hand glided hesitantly, curiously, gratefully over the richly different textures of his legs and torso—over soft, straight hairs and tight, curly hairs; over taut, deep-tanned skin and kid-glove unexposed skin.

"You're right about the bed, Leda," he said in a low, shaky voice. "It does float."

His fingers had resumed a focused assault on her most secret nerve endings. "Oh, Nat . . ." she whispered.

He smoothed the hair back from her face, poring over her with searching, aching tenderness until she could no longer bear not to taste his lips, and she pulled him toward her in a deep, longing kiss. And then she felt his hands underneath her bottom, lifting her slightly, edging one of her legs away with the side of his knee, murmuring her name once, and then again.

For an endless moment she held her breath, hearing nothing but the knocking of her heart, seeing nothing but a bright green blaze of light behind her eyelids, feeling nothing but a kind of expanding endlessness as he pressed her hips to his. Where her tongue ended and his began; where the boundaries of her body were drawn, and his, she neither knew nor cared. All she understood was that they had been thrown together into a crucible, melted and fused into a nugget of bright, pure gold. Leda had found, by purest chance, the secret that had eluded all the alchemists of all the ages; the secret that had eluded her, until now.

Hugging the knowledge to her heart, she found herself borne

higher and higher on the tip of a breaking wave; and then, when she felt she could no longer keep so much joy secret, the wave broke over her, bathing her cheeks, her breasts, her arms with pulsating pleasure, and releasing her at last.

She and Nat were washed up ashore together, clinging to one another, breathing heavily, two pebbles tumbled onto a beach by crashing surf. For a long while they lay collapsed in each other's arms, Nat on his back, Leda across his chest, as he stroked and petted her hair in an oddly protective way.

"Any broken bones, love?" he murmured, hugging her to him. "I've never held anyone so tightly in all my life."

"Now that you mention it," she said, nuzzling the skin just below his ear, "I do feel strangely boneless at the moment. Do you suppose they all just melted?" she asked, dropping little kisses alternately with tiny nips along his neck.

He raised the arm she had draped across his chest and let it fall, with a plop, back across him. "Hmm. A serious case," he intoned. "However, I shouldn't worry too much. It's a scientifically proven fact that bones grow back after a good night's rest."

Glancing down the full length of his body, she said wickedly, "Are you sure, Captain, that it takes quite that long?"

He grinned sheepishly and dropped a light kiss on the tip of her nose. "*You,* witch; *you're* the reason it's so damned hard to get a good night's rest." With a sweeping motion he rolled her over on top of him, raiding her mouth hungrily, one hand pinning her hips to his unyielding body, the other hand twining in the tangles of her hair, murmuring words of love between wet, possessive kisses.

"Ah, Leda," he growled hoarsely, "how do I get you out of my system? What does it take?" he asked in frustration.

"It takes two, Captain," she answered with a moan of pleasure, wondering how she had lived before she'd met him, and how she'd survive when he sailed away the next day.

The sun was not yet slanting into the Red Cottage when Leda began to be dragged groggily toward consciousness.

"Hey. Sleepyhead," Nat whispered into her ear, kissing her temple and brushing away a wisp of hair that clung to it. "Are you awake?"

"Mmmnph-hmnph." She could not, try as she might, will her eyelids to open.

"Darlin', I've got to go," he said softly, sitting next to her on the bed, petting her hair with short, tender strokes. "We've got to sail the *Swan* to Kingston, stock up on groceries, pick up an engine part. Leda? Are you asleep?"

"Mmmn-mmmn," she answered, pivoting her head, on her nose, from side to side across her pillow. "Timezit," she mumbled.

"Nearly dawn. Look, Leda, we both fell asleep so quickly last night after . . . I didn't get the chance to tell you . . . Leda?"

She wanted to tell him profound truths, too, but in her half-wakened state it didn't seem possible. Instead she settled on a sleepy I-love-you smile. And then she was dreamily aware that he was gently pulling the sheet up over her bare shoulders and reaching down to drop one more kiss on her brow. She was drowsily aware of his scratchy beard, and of the faint scent of his brand of cheroot. And then she heard—or thought she heard—him softly mutter, "I want you with me, you chucklehead." Then he was gone, and she drifted back to sleep. But when she did awake it was with a jolt. She hadn't dreamt it! He had gone!

And this time it was for two miserable weeks. Whoever thought up the two-week charter should be beheaded, she fumed, working herself into an exquisite rage of frustration. It would be fourteen days before she would hold him in her arms again, hear his voice, laugh with him. Three hundred and thirty-six hours before she could tell him that she loved him. She had wanted to say so last night, but the words wouldn't come; she didn't want to embarrass Nat, put him in the awkward situation of having to respond. It seemed so trite and old-fashioned to say "I love you" just because you happened to be making love. Well, too bad; Leda was trite and old-fashioned.

And besides, now she couldn't help wondering if he would have said "I love you" back.

At her desk later she doodled listlessly. Twenty thousand, one hundred and sixty minutes, minimum, before she'd know the answer to the question "Do you love me?" Because if he didn't volunteer an opinion, she was going to ask him outright. If he said no . . . if he said no, could she spend a week with him, in confined quarters, trying not to burst into tears every minute? On second thought, it was better *not* to ask outright.

Still later, Leda dragged her bare feet through the warm sand on a sunset walk along Princess Margaret Beach. She had calculated that by the time she'd counted slowly to 1,209,600, he would be back, and she could ask him outright. Because it was better to know. If he didn't love her . . . well, he was selling the *Swan,* anyway; the problem would take care of itself. If he did love her—which, of course, he didn't, or he would have said so last night—but if he *did* . . .

She plopped down on the sand, staring into the still-blinding sunset, closing her eyes tightly, seeing sun-balls dance across the inside of her eyelids. If he did love her—so what? There was still the question of compatibility. Sexually, there was no problem; definitely, they were compatible. But did they both want the same things from life? She drew a childish rendition of a sailboat in the hard, damp sand with a stick, then drew a large box around the boat, with a roof, and a little smoking chimney on top of the roof.

She had always had a precise idea of what she wanted: a job that was exciting and challenging, first of all. And then eventually, she'd fall in love, settle down, have a baby or two. Maine would be a nice place to live. She saw no difficulty in juggling a career in brokerage with a family. Her husband, of course, would be successful at a career he loved. That was the plan; a reasonable plan.

Instead she'd fallen for a high-seas drifter who regarded women and children with about the same enthusiasm as the Ancient Mariner regarded the albatross around his neck. And now Nat was even bored with chartering, bored with the *Swan.*

He wanted a smaller, simpler boat, one that presumably he could sail himself—the rest of the way around the world. Wonderful. She sure knew how to pick them. Why couldn't she have fallen in love with someone more practical—like an astronaut, or the President of the United States?

Smiling glumly, she poked her stick into the sand, making little portholes in the boat. Looked at one way, Nat could be viewed as idle, selfish, egotistical, and without ambition. But looked at another way, he was conscientious, tender, sensitive—and without ambition. She sighed heavily. There was no getting around it; he was aimless. It was the chief source of their incompatibility.

And yet, while she couldn't easily imagine him behind a picket fence, trimming rosebushes, she *could* imagine him, oh, doing lots of things. Wiping dishes, rowing her ashore, going for a long walk on a beach, bouncing a baby on his knee, teaching a young child to take the helm of a sailboat. She shook the fantasies out of her head; they made no sense. Or did they? Her emotions had told her, before her mind had, that Nat Hardy would make a loving husband, a wonderful father. If he insisted on fulfilling his dream to sail around the world, fine. But she was going too.

Leda stood up and brushed the sand off the back of her legs. It was dark; she'd been lost in a revery for . . . how long? For about four thousand five hundred seconds. A moment of delicious panic seized her. Before she knew it, he'd be back, and she hadn't even thought about a menu, come up with a provisions list, decided what to pack, familiarized herself with the nearby islands . . .

CHAPTER NINE

Leda was on her knees, digging frantically through a wicker basket of bikinis at the tiny boutique in Port Elizabeth. The black one was too small. The red one was a knockout but . . . wrong color. The blue one with the brass buckles . . . pretty . . . but where was the top? That one did not come with a top, she learned; it was a "monokini."

This was ridiculous. She still had an urgent letter to write; a cable to answer; her call to Antigua hadn't been returned; Julie was coming down with a cold; Nat would return any hour now; and here she was, poking around like a shopper from *The Love Boat*. Still, she had to have a bikini; the red one would have to do. Leda threw her money on the counter, snatched up her package, and dashed out of the boutique, straight into the arms of an irate-looking blackbeard.

"Nat! How did you know where I was?" she asked, irrationally horrified.

"Julie told me, obviously. For God's sake, Leda, you're supposed to be packed and ready on your doorstep. What can you possibly need from a boutique?" His voice was tense, his face haggard and exhausted.

"Uh-h . . . suntan lotion." She clenched the bag tightly in one hand as she allowed herself to be hauled away abruptly by the other.

"I've got all that on board," he growled. "What I don't have is a crew. Where're your things?"

"In the Cottage," she gasped, flying alongside him. "First I've got to type—explain—a couple of things to Julie. You look terrible," she blurted.

"Why, thank you, ma'm," he drawled, and then added tiredly, "I've just sailed all night from Trinidad."

"Trinidad? I thought you were taking the charter group *north."*

"Juanita talked them into going south instead; she wanted to see some friends in Trinidad before heading home to Brazil. It was reasonable," he added resignedly. "Juanita stayed in Trinidad, the charterers flew back home from there, and I deadheaded back."

"You sailed the *Swan* yourself? All night long?" It seemed a reckless, stupid thing to do, and she was suddenly furious with him for doing it. "No wonder you look terrible," she fumed.

His laugh was short and tired. "It's not as dramatic as it sounds. I had the *Swan* on the autopilot, and I slept in ten-minute snatches; there wasn't much traffic in the shipping lanes. Besides," he said, putting his arm around her and giving her a quick squeeze, "my dreams are a hell of a lot sexier when I catnap. I missed you, darlin'."

They were at her office. "I'll get your bags and meet you here in five minutes," he said. "Now *move*, mate." He took her by the shoulders and gave her a brisk shove through the door.

By the end of the next half hour they had weighed anchor, raised sail, and were on their way to Kingston in St. Vincent for provisions. The need for frenzied haste was over for the moment—the *Swan* was sailing as fast as it possibly could—and Leda had time to reflect that it was sunny, that it was Saturday, and that she was alone on the ocean with Nat Hardy. And later, once they'd stocked up on groceries, there'd be nothing to do but enjoy, until the Stevensons arrived on Sunday afternoon.

The *Swan* heeled over to port in the strong trade wind breeze, and Leda braced her foot on a cockpit seat as she held the big steering wheel effortlessly in her hands. The boat was beautifully balanced; she had sailed smaller boats that took far more strength and concentration. There was little to do but count the flying fish that skimmed from whitecap to whitecap, and take deep, restoring breaths of the clean, clear air. Incredible that she hadn't been sailing since she arrived in Bequia!

146

"Hey, Captain!" she called down cheerfully to Nat as she caught a glimpse of him near the hatchway.

Still below, he looked out, folded his arms across the top step of the companionway, and smiled. "Yeah, squirt?"

"How about throwing my visor up to me? It's in my duffel bag." Just then a whitecap slapped up against the hull and spilled over onto her, drenching her T-shirt with salty spray. "Ya-a-aghh," she cried, *that* wave had my name on it. Now if this were New England, I'd be frozen stiff now," she laughed, deliriously happy that it wasn't. She was wearing his "It's Better in Bequia" shirt—and it was.

"I'll take the wheel while you come below and get out of the shorts and shirt and into a swimsuit," he offered, starting up the steps.

She held up her hand to stop him. She'd packed only the red bikini, which she suddenly decided was an idiotic garment; New Englanders did not wear red bikinis. "I'd rather just steer for a while, Nat." She smiled happily.

"And I'd rather *no* one steered for a while," he said, handing her the visor and lazily trailing his look over her wet, clinging T-shirt. "Suppose we put the *Swan* on autopilot," he drawled, flipping a switch and causing the wheel to turn without Leda's help. "And then"—he yawned—"we can take a little nap."

"A nap, huh? Who's going to watch for ships and killer whales?" she challenged, standing and stretching her legs, which had become stiff from bracing.

"You are, love. What I meant was, *I'm* going to take a nap," he said, pulling her down beside him on the white-cushioned cockpit seat. "This is my favorite spot—dry, warm, and you can see where you're going." Stretching out full length on his stomach, he nuzzled his head on her lap, his warm breath heating the inside of her thighs. He sighed drowsily. "I think I've just found a better favorite spot. . . ."

Leda gazed at his tanned cheek, at the tiny white lines fanning out from his closed eyes, and idly smoothed his salt-encrusted hair. His arm lay limp across her knees, the black curled hairs also white with salt. His shorts, his shirt—everything showed the salty evidence of a hard sail to Bequia. A feeling of almost aching tenderness flowed through her as she closed her eyes in the bright Caribbean sunshine, feeling the warm wind lift and tease the wispy tendrils that had come loose from her thick single braid. The *Swan* rose and plunged with a steady, powerful motion through the rolling seas. She felt as though she had come home. There were no neighbors, no streets, no traffic lights, but *home is where the heart is,* she told herself.

Bending over, she dropped a gentle kiss on his salty brow. "You taste like a pretzel," she murmured. Now, should she tell him? Tell him that she loved him? But he didn't answer; he was asleep, breathing deeply and peacefully, and Leda, hazily enchanted herself, let him sleep on for another hour. When he awoke, the smile came first, and then the opened eyes.

"You act as though you're used to waking up in women's laps," she prompted, fighting a jealous twinge in her breast. She *had* to get over this possessiveness!

"I was dreaming that I was lying in clover," he said, sounding a little surprised. "There were mountains around, and a noisy brook. The brook part I understand—listen to the sound of the water gurgling along the hull—but mountains?" He had shifted onto his back, gazing up at her, touching her cheek, her hair.

"Mount Soufrière on St. Vincent is ahead," she said. "Were the dream-mountains volcanic?"

"No, they were more like your Rocky Mountains, surrounded by huge expanses of land. Why would I dream about that?" He stared up at her rather blankly, as though she should have known the answer.

"Could it be that you're ready to swallow the anchor and move ashore, sailorman?" Her voice was low, almost beseeching.

"And give all this up?" he asked incredulously.

Her heart bounced lopsidedly in her chest. "Give all what up?"

He swung an arm out toward the sky and dropped it into a sweeping motion along the boat. "That. This. You."

"And in another week? What then?" she said softly.

He sat up abruptly, his back to her. "I don't plan that far ahead." Glancing at the compass he said quickly, "We've altered course."

"Yes," she said, surprised at his sudden change of mood. "The current was setting us too far to the west; I adjusted the autopilot a little. I didn't want to wake you."

He ran his hand through his stiff, salty hair, still groggy and tired-looking. Several emotions marched across his brow: uncertainty, peevishness, surprise. Speaking slowly, choosing his words carefully, he said, "I'm a little surprised, that's all. Juanita would never have altered course without waking me first."

Embarrassed, she answered quietly, "We are on course now, aren't we?"

"Well, yes, but Juanita would've wakened me," he insisted petulantly.

She rose and stretched her arms down toward her feet; everything was stiff and sore from her effort not to move and wake him. "I'm not Juanita, Nat," she said without looking at him.

"So it seems." He cleared his throat. "Leda, wake me up the next time, would you?"

"Yes, *sir,*" she said, snapping to attention with a smart salute. "Permission to go below, *sir.* Permission to take a tour, *sir.* Please, Nat?" she smiled, relenting in her sarcasm as the look on his face darkened.

The cloud passed as quickly as it had gathered. "I forgot— you haven't had a chance to see anything, have you?" he asked, taking one last look on deck before preceding her down the companionway steps.

"How come you're not all eager to show off your yacht, like Gerald Rafferty with his *Moonraker?*" They were standing in the after cabin, obviously the captain's quarters, and Leda was glancing around with lively interest at the snug, neat bunks—a

149

single berth on the starboard side, a double on the port side. She wondered which side Juanita slept on.

"Gerald Rafferty has a yacht to show off," he answered. "But the *Swan* is just a toy, a plaything for charterers. It's too modern, too . . . I don't know. I've just never taken to it."

Leda held onto a grab rail, taking in the quietly expert woodwork, the subdued navy-blue berth cushions, and the little blue throw pillows, each with a graceful, stylized white swan appliquéd on the front. "I think the cabin is beautiful, Nat," she said. "And look at your navigator's desk! It looks like the cockpit of a Boeing 747," she marveled, running her hands lightly over dozens of circuits, switches, and knobs.

"Most of the electronics are unnecessary," he said flatly. "My father sailed around the world without any of these gadgets."

She lifted the slanted desktop, expecting to see a pile of navigation charts stored there. Instead she found a blueprint of an automobile chassis, and sketches of dashboard panels and sleek, futuristic profiles of sports cars, all executed in a neat architect's hand and signed and dated by Nat Hardy. "Nat! I didn't know you did design work. Not . . . not that it's any of my business if you do or not," she added.

Arms folded, he was bracing himself effortlessly against a beautifully scaled-down chest of drawers. "But it *is* your business, more than you know. I lie awake at night, thinking of you —sometimes for hours," he said, his gaze lingering on the contours of her still-damp shirt. "Occasionally a little of that restlessness goes into a design idea. When that happens"—he shrugged—"I get up, sit down at my desk, and work out a rough sketch. In some odd, unexplained way you've started my creative juices flowing again."

There he goes again, she thought dizzily, *playing Ping-Pong with my emotions.* One minute he was keeping her at arm's length, fighting for his independence, resisting any suggestion of making a commitment; the next, he was dropping little heart-stopping revelations like these. It wasn't fair. She stared at him in bewilderment, clutching the grab rail, trying to keep her balance in the increasingly rough seas.

"I think I'll have to adjust our course again," he said, steadying himself. "We'll head as high as we can for another—"

A big wave swept under them, rolling the boat on its ear and throwing Leda into his arms. "Now I call this fate," he murmured, folding his arms around her. "And yet I was so determined to keep this trip strictly business; I didn't want either of us remembering that we were man and woman instead of captain and crew."

"Got any more bright ideas, Captain?" She sighed, lifting her face to meet his with a dreamy smile.

"Oh, one or two," he said, cupping her chin in the palm of his hand and lowering his mouth to hers in a kiss that was agonizingly overdue.

Another wave rolled over the *Swan,* upsetting their kiss. "Wow"—she giggled—"when they talk about the earth moving, do they include the ocean too?"

He gave her braid a little yank, then said, "Have a look around at the rest of the boat while I go on deck and check things. You'll see what I mean by 'toy.' "

Slowly making her way forward through the pitching boat, Leda was surprised to see that the main cabin was designed in complete contrast to Nat's private cabin.

Instead of warm walnut and a traditional blue color scheme, the effect was almost monochromatic. The deep-tufted cushions were covered in silver-gray synthetic suede. Smoky acrylic doors enclosed all the cabinets, including a large liquor locker. An ice-cube maker, and spigots marked SCOTCH and RUM suggested that bartending was an important responsibility on a charter boat.

The thick pile carpet was a pale oyster shade, which struck Leda as slightly insane, considering the rough-and-tumble use a boat got. Next to the house-sized stereo opposite the bar section were two swivel lounge chairs in black Naugahyde mounted on chrome-plated columns bolted to the floor. Everything was cool, sophisticated, impersonal. Nat was right; it wasn't the kind of boat you could love.

Leda groped her way past two ultramodern guest staterooms,

151

into a tiny cabin, all the way in the bow, that interested her very much. A brass "crew" plaque was screwed to the door. A narrow bunk covered in a colorful striped fabric vied for space with a small porcelain washbasin and toilet, a closet, and two or three drawers. Tacked to the louvered closet door was a checklist of reminders which began, "Have drinks and hors d'oeuvres ready on arrival." Leda read through it avidly—she knew nothing about professional crewing, she realized now—before noticing a small tortoiseshell comb with inlaid turquoise left behind in the corner of a shelf below the checklist. It had to be Juanita's.

So Juanita had stayed in her own cabin, way up here, after all. Leda fingered the pretty trinket thoughtfully. She'd realized before this, of course, that Nat was too fiercely independent to risk getting involved with Juanita. What she didn't know, even now, was why he was so fiercely independent. Surely not just because he was an item in the *London Times* after his failed circumnavigation attempt? That wasn't reason enough—even for a man as proud as Nat Hardy. Leda believed too much in his character, in his integrity, to think he'd shun a permanent relationship just because his vanity had been wounded.

The boat reared and plunged, more wildly this time. The motion was nearly unbearable this far forward; but then, hired crew would hardly be favored with the most comfortable part of the boat. Hanging on to the bunkboard, Leda lifted and fell with the boat's motion. Sometimes her stomach came along, but sometimes it didn't. She found herself feeling not well. Feeling very unwell. Her stomach flopping over ominously, Leda made a beeline for the fresh air on deck.

"Gad, Leda, you look green as a parakeet. Feeling a touch of *mal de mer?*" Nat asked politely.

She managed a limp smile. "Me? Not a chance. Cast-iron stomach. Ah . . . so pleasant up here," she said, drawing her lungs full of sunshine and salt air. "Will we be much, uh, longer, do you think?"

His smile was surprisingly sympathetic for a disgustingly fit-looking person. "Here, take the wheel again. Stare at the horizon to get your sense of balance back. You'll feel better in a minute."

The technique was effective; her nausea passed quickly, and in no time Leda was humming a light sailor's ditty to herself, content to be sitting, without conversation, next to Nat.

"Damn," he said, under his breath, running his finger lightly over the curve of her breast through the damp T-shirt. "I wish we didn't have to pick up the charter tomorrow."

"Captain, *sir,*" she teased. "Do you want me . . . ohh-ho . . . to steer a straight course or not?"

He sighed in resignation. "We've got to drop the sails soon, anyway. Then we'll power into the harbor, dash ashore for groceries, and stow everything. Scrubbing, waxing, polishing the brass—that should take three or four hours, tops. We should be finished with the work by sundown," he said wearily.

"It all sounds so glamorous," she said ironically. "Nat, why do you do it?" The question had been on her mind for weeks. "Obviously you don't have to charter the *Swan.*"

He'd lit a cheroot, his first of the day, and his face had settled, despite his sun-squint, into an expression of repose. "Do you want the socially acceptable answer—'I do it for the tax write-off'—or the real one?"

"What do *you* think, Captain?" she asked him quietly in return.

"I think the real answer sounds a little idiotic." He took a deep drag on his cigar and exhaled. "The real reason I've been taking charters is to keep a perspective on things. When you're comfortably off," he said dryly, "it gets easier and easier to forget that other people weren't put on the planet just to serve your needs. There's an irresistible tendency to take people for granted. But when I charter I have to be butler, chauffeur, mechanic, and all-around hired lackey. Chartering"—he winked affectionately—"keeps me humble."

Nat Hardy, deliberately practicing humility? "You make it sound like a penance," she said, astounded at his answer.

"That, slave, will depend entirely on the Stevensons. Come on, let's get these sails down."

Approximately three million boxes of food stood piled onto every square inch of flat surface in the main cabin of the *Swan*. Nat was stowing cans, bottles, boxes, every conceivable form of food. Leda polished the brass and tried, undoubtedly in vain, to memorize which cabinets held what food.

"Nobody can eat that much food in a week," she insisted, buffing a kerosene lamp into a satiny sheen. "*Or* a month."

"Okay, I got a little carried away," Nat conceded. "It's part of my pack-rat mentality. But if the Stevensons *do* buy the *Swan,* I'll have to hire and feed a delivery crew all the way back to Florida. It's a little-known fact, but a typical one-hundred-eighty-pound male, while at sea, eats his own weight in food every three days."

"No kidding?" she said absently.

"Yes, *kidding,* you lummox. What're you daydreaming about?"

She was sitting at her allotted little square of the dining table, staring blankly at four more kerosene lamps, a clock, a barometer, and three ashtrays. All brass. All unpolished. "Oh, I wasn't *thinking* about anything, really. Just . . . feeling, I guess."

"Feeling what?" He was on his knees, packing canned tomato juice into some hidden recess under the galley sink.

Leda stood up, folded her arms across a pile of boxes stacked chest-high, rested her chin on her hands, and gazed down at him. "Feeling undesired, I guess. Chartering seems perilously like work. I somehow thought, today at least, that we'd have some time?"

He leaned back on his calves and smiled lazily at her. "Well, since you look at me *that* way. What'd you have in mind?" he drawled, rising and standing on the other side of the stack of boxes, folding his hands over hers.

She demurely lowered her gaze from his. "One possibility would be a quick game of checkers," she suggested, carefully serious.

He considered. "Somehow, I don't really have a taste for checkers. Anything else?" he asked softly, rubbing the inside of

154

her wrist with one of his thumbs, then lifting it to his tongue and casually raising Leda's body temperature six or seven degrees.

She raised her impishly clear green eyes to his smoldering look. "We could always take a whack at one of them or-gees I hear the *Swan*'s famous for."

"Just the two of us? Shouldn't I invite more?" he asked, tickling the inside bend of her elbow with his tongue.

"Gee, I dunno," she hedged, looking around the cabin appraisingly. "Think we can feed them all? Maybe we'd better just keep it simple." She laughed from deep inside her throat as his tongue continued to turn her every thought into warm, sweet honey.

"Of course, this isn't the way I'd planned it," he murmured huskily, tonguing the ultrasensitive area between her ear and her shoulder. "I'd planned to finish the chores and have hors d'oeuvres at sundown—"

"It's already dark out," she interrupted.

"I'd planned champagne, a shower. . . ." He ran his tongue lightly around her earlobe.

"And instead," she gasped, "the chores aren't done, and we're hot, and tired . . ."

". . . and sweaty . . . salty . . ." Nat's mouth came around to hers in a sudden, searing kiss, almost wanton in its urgency, his tongue plundering the dark recesses of her mouth, demanding and fierce, as he pulled her T-shirt up over her breasts, one arm holding her to his damp, bare chest. He unzipped the back of her shorts; his fingers slid underneath the denim constraint, underneath the gossamer fabric of her panties, artfully, masterfully working their sorcery on her.

Leda's response was instantaneous, electrifying. Before she had time to consider, before she had time to drink in the sliding sweetness of his mouth, she collapsed in gasping surrender against him, barely able to stand, even with his arm supporting her. For a dizzying moment she leaned against him, panting quickly and heavily, shocked at the intensity of her satisfaction. "I . . . this isn't the way I had planned it, either," she gasped.

"Leda, you are coming with me," he said, his voice rough and unsteady, lifting her, with her T-shirt still rolled above her breasts, her shorts around her knees; lifting her and carrying her in his arms through the boxes, through the clutter, into his cabin; laying her, still half-dazed, on the double berth; pulling off his shorts and her clothing carelessly and rekindling her desire with quick, concentrated licks of flame before his swift, low rush into her body; raining furious, unrestrained kisses on her mouth; and finally, with a sharp gasp of his own, sliding into quiescence, slippery with heat, on top of her.

They lay together, tangled in one another's arms and legs, limp with heat and love, for a long moment.

"Say," Leda murmured through a haze of satisfied pleasure, "aren't orgies supposed to last longer?"

"I think it depends a lot on how many you've been to, recently." He had raised himself up on one elbow and was lifting free the wispy strands of hair that were caught in the dampness of her neck. "What's *your* calendar been like?"

"Slow," she admitted.

"Mine too." He smiled. "Seems a bit of a waste, doesn't it?"

"Mmmm," she agreed dreamily, wondering whether she could just pay to stay on board as a charter customer after next week. Three thousand dollars a week, fifty-two weeks a year—it would definitely strain her budget, she decided ruefully.

His lips were drifting in a gentle caress from her temple, across her cheek, to the corner of her slightly swollen lips. "You're so good for me, Leda," he said quietly. And then he laughed. "Or maybe not so good. My motto has always been 'First, the ship.' But just now I find myself thinking, 'First, a shower. Tomorrow, the damn ship.' How about you?"

"A shower sounds heavenly." She sighed. "Make that two."

"And waste all that water? I have a better idea."

And he did. "A yacht's supply of water isn't infinite, you know," he explained patiently as he lathered a bar of soap briskly between his hands. "That's the only reason we're showering together, of course," he added, adjusting the shower spray precisely over Leda's head.

156

"Of course," she sputtered, basking in the stream of warm water.

"Too hot? It seems hot to me," he said judiciously, soaping and briskly massaging Leda's back. "On the other hand, I've been taking nothing but cold showers for the last two weeks. What do I know? Tonight, miss, we're featuring a complimentary shampoo," he babbled on cheerfully. "Would you be interested?"

"For free? Sure." She laughed weakly. His hands had soaped their way around to Leda's front and were scrubbing her breasts and throat scientifically—yet not scientifically at all.

He made a grand show of reading the contents of the shampoo label. "Our own special blend of the finest herbs: nutmeg, cinnamon, coriander, honey, oil of avocado and—this is what sets us apart—a pinch of saffron. Right, then, here we go."

And he rubbed and lathered her scalp with his maestro's touch until she felt squeaky clean down to the last follicle. Clean, rinsed, relaxed, and lazily interested again. Really, it was almost embarrassing.

"Okay, Captain, now you," she said, slapping a bar of soap onto his chest and rubbing and circling into the black curly hairs there. "I bet I can do you in less than a gallon of water," she said breezily, working the lather over his ribs, his midriff, then down over his lower belly. . . .

His forearms were resting on her shoulders as he said in a smiling but unsteady voice, "By the way, have I explained what this little molded-in shower seat is for? It's so that one can sit down during the shower and . . . and wash the soles of one's feet, for example. There are other uses, too. Here, let me show you. . . ."

CHAPTER TEN

From the cockpit of the *Swan,* Leda scanned the Young Island dock, left to right, right to left, with her binoculars. It was Nat, all right, loading a large suitcase into his flat-bottom dinghy. Then another, smaller suitcase. Then two duffel bags. And a shopping bag. Now a man in long pants and a long-sleeved shirt, rolled up, and a jacket tossed over his shoulder, was climbing in. And after him, a woman in white pants and a hot-pink blouse, holding something in her arms. Now the woman was climbing back out onto the dock again. Then back into the skiff, again holding something in her arms. Oops. Out again. In again. One more time and Nat would throw her in the harbor, Leda felt sure. But no; whatever the problem was, it was under control. Nat jumped into the skiff and it roared away from the dock toward the *Swan.* Leda's maiden charter was under way.

Whipping out Juanita's old charter checklist, Leda reread the part about having drinks and hors d'oeuvres ready. They were ready. In between polishing and waxing all morning, Leda had worked frantically in the sweltering galley—over Nat's objections—preparing an elaborate assortment of hors d'oeuvres for the Stevensons. The small table in the cockpit, shaded by an awning overhead, was buried under a tantalizing selection of Caribbean specialties: shrimp-stuffed avocados; lobster quiche; crab dip, clam dip, oyster dip; slabs of cheese and bushels of crackers. Down below, a bowl of codfish fritter batter stood ready for deep-frying. Probably Leda had overdone her preparations. Nat thought so. What if they wanted to get under way immediately, he'd said. What if they weren't hungry, he'd said. Make something simple and refreshing, he'd urged her. And darn it—he was right. Leda was faint and irritable from the heat and cooking, and very tense.

Still, as she stood on deck, cooling down in the trade wind breeze while she put the finishing touches to the table, she felt pleased with the professional, catered look she'd achieved. Whether it was worth having to jump out of Nat's arms that morning, perhaps the last one she'd ever spend with him . . . She pushed the thought from her mind; it was unbearable.

The roar of Nat's outboard drew nearer, and Leda positioned herself at the gate on deck, ready for inspection. An hour ago Nat had mocked her unnecessary formality when she changed into khaki shorts and a dark-blue polo shirt, the universally recognized uniform of a crewmember aboard a yacht.

What *was* she trying to prove, anyway? That she could be a crack crew? Who cared? Certainly not Nat. That she followed orders—oh, definitely he cared about that. *Yessir, nosir, anything you say, sir.* As long as she left the decisions to him. As long as she didn't adjust the compass course or try to force him to come to terms with his feelings for her . . .

"Well, here they are, Leda," Nat said from his skiff, helping the woman in it over the mountain of luggage. "Mark and Wilhelmina Stevenson and . . . Tippy." Nat's eyes held Leda's in a look of ironic amusement. "Tippy wasn't convinced he wanted to go on this charter."

"So nice to meet you," Mrs. Stevenson said formally, handing up an unhappy-looking small black dog. "Tippy can be so silly. He isn't all that fond of sailboats, but I've never seen him so hostile before. Certainly he's never *bitten* anyone before. I'm very sorry about that, Captain Hardy," she said over her shoulder, expertly climbing the boarding ladder and immediately reclaiming her dog, who had begun to whimper in Leda's arms.

"Don't mention it," Nat said with a grim smile, rubbing his forearm. "I'd forgotten all about it. I shouldn't have lunged for him so suddenly when he ran out of the skiff the first time."

"Dog's a damn pest, of course," muttered Mark Stevenson. He was a man of about sixty, heavily built and sweating profusely. "I could use a drink."

"Certainly, Mr. Stevenson," Leda said with a khaki-and-navy smile. "Why don't you just relax under the awning and cool down while I stow your bags? Or would you prefer to see your cabin first? Or would you perhaps like to go for a dip? Of course, you might prefer a shower. . . ."

"I said I could use a damn *drink,*" Stevenson interrupted her.

"Yes. You did, didn't you. What would you like?" Leda asked him coolly, her eager desire to please suddenly dampened.

"Know how to make a rum flip?" he asked her with a suspicious look. He might have been asking her where she was on the day of a particular murder.

"A rum flip? Certainly," she answered breezily. Actually, Leda hadn't a clue how to make a rum flip, but she remembered seeing the quaint name in a recipe book in the galley. "May I get you something to drink, Mrs. Stevenson?" she asked politely.

"A bowl of cold water, please," the woman answered promptly. In answer to Leda's blank look she added, "For *Tippy.* I'll have a lime daiquiri, if it's no bother."

"Fine. In the meantime why don't you just help yourself," Leda suggested, modestly indicating the elegant repast with a sweep of her hand.

Unlike her husband, Wilhelmina definitely seemed more interested in food than in drink. Lowering Tippy to the deck, she cooed, "Let me just take a peek before I wash up. Everything looks so . . ." she began, and then she paused. ". . . so much like shellfish. This is mostly *shellfish,*" she repeated, horrified.

Leda's heart sank. Nat was coming up the companionway steps for more luggage; she threw him a dismayed look. "Is there something wrong with shellfish?"

"I'm allergic to it, that's all," Mrs. Stevenson sniffed. "As I indicated in your diet-preference questionnaire."

"But you never returned it," Leda objected faintly. "We just assumed—"

"You may not have received it; I *certainly* returned it."

"Mina," her husband interrupted, "just drop it. There's plenty of other food. Now. What about the rum flip?"

Grateful for the diversion, Leda said, "Coming right up." As she dove down the steps, upset and embarrassed, Nat said quietly to her, "The simple syrup is in the fridge."

Simple syrup? What was he talking about? Sixty seconds later, she knew. A rum flip called for a boiled and cooled sugarwater concoction; thank goodness the *Swan* had a supply. Leda added eggs and ice to the cocktail shaker and shook it furiously, wondering where the missing questionnaire was. Nat came up behind her, slipping an arm lightly around her waist, and she jumped. "Oh! Sorry. I was preoccupied," she apologized, instantly aware that she'd missed his touch in the last couple of hours.

"How're you feeling, slave?" he asked sympathetically, brushing her cheek with his lips.

"Humble," she said grimly. "Nat, would you mind taking up that bowl of water for Tippy?"

"Cheer up"—he grinned—"Stevenson looks like he'll mellow out a lot. *She's* probably hopeless, though. Don't forget the grated nutmeg. I love you." And he was back up the steps before she turned, stunned, and said, "Where's . . . the nutmeg?"

Loved her? What a bizarre sense of timing the man had! How could he . . . how would she . . . *loved* her! Did he mean that? Was it an offhand remark, meant to cheer? Should she ask? Now? Later? The situation was insane. Now, of all times, they needed a moment alone. Now, of all times, their lives were not their own. Distractedly she poured out two rum flips and brought them up on deck, where Nat was charming Mark Stevenson with a sea yarn about the *Swan*. Mrs. Stevenson was dividing her time between Tippy, who was barking noisily at a passing dinghy, and the non-allergenic snacks.

Stevenson took one look at his drink and said, "No nutmeg?"

"I thought I'd check to be sure," Leda lied, recovering. Then, remembering his wife's daiquiri request, Leda foisted the second rum drink onto Nat, dashed back down, brought up the nutmeg grater, dashed down again, made up a whole pitcher of daiquiris, decided to postpone the deep-fry, and came back up on deck, harried and breathless after thirty-three minutes of chartering. Her respect for Juanita was growing.

"Gracious. The sun is so blinding," Wilhelmina murmured in a distressed tone.

"Perhaps you'd like a visor," Nat suggested. "We have a supply of them."

"Oh, no; my sunglasses, I think. They're in my handbag." She looked expectantly at Leda.

"Would you like me to fetch it for you?" Leda asked, feeling a deep kinship with Tippy.

"Would you?"

"Certainly." Down again, up on deck again, with the handbag.

"Thank you *so* much. I . . . oh, naughty Tippy. Not already." Wilhelmina shook a jeweled finger at the little black terrier, who was standing at the gate looking down into the skiff tied alongside the *Swan,* then at his mistress, his tail wagging furiously.

"I'm afraid, Captain Hardy, that Tippy's kidneys aren't what they used to be. I'm sure it's all the excitement so far; he'll settle down. But, would you mind just running the poor dear ashore for his little walk? I'll go along with you, if you think Tippy will be a problem to handle."

Nat's laugh was a half-snort. "I think I can handle it," he said, rising and pulling his yachting cap farther down over his eyes and obscuring the look of impatience that had settled there.

Mark Stevenson stared at his wife, aghast. "For God's sake, Mina, Hardy and I were just getting down to business. There's a lot about this vessel I want to know. Surely the girl can take Tippy ashore."

"But she's only a . . . Well," she checked herself, "does she know how to operate the skiff?"

"As well as I do, ma'm," Nat answered dryly.

Nothing like being a liberated slave, Leda thought, gathering up the dog and climbing down into the small boat. She was about to cast off the lines, when she thought better of it and

162

cautiously turned the ignition. It caught hard, but it started. Then she threw off the lines, backed the skiff away from the *Swan,* and headed for shore. She'd never operated Nat's skiff before and was immoderately pleased in his confidence in her.

Ashore, she tried hard to convince herself that Nat's "I love you" was not intended seriously. She tried but she failed. Whenever Leda was happy she became restless, almost hyperactive. Right now, she'd have liked nothing better than to run and splash along the beach barefoot, but she settled for giving herself two or three tight little hugs as she rocked back and forth on her feet, waiting for Tippy.

By the time she had the terrier back aboard the *Swan,* Tippy's mistress was indulging in a little swim, carefully keeping her elaborate hairdo above water. The men were deep in conversation, Mr. Stevenson having taken possession of the cocktail shaker. When Nat saw Leda approach, he excused himself with the suggestion that he and Leda needed to go over a few things before weighing anchor.

He led Leda below to his cabin, shutting the companionway door behind them, and rolled out a chart of the area. "We'll be doing the usual islands: back to Bequia, then to Mustique, Union, Palm, PSV, and the Tobago Cays, of course. Besides shellfish, the woman's allergic to most brands of suntan lotion; don't go near her with ours. She hates coconut, the smell of bourbon, and the color red; all were listed on that lost questionnaire. It's reasonable to assume that she's jealous of you; her husband's been trotting after you with his eyes—"

"I didn't notice that!"

"But I did, so avoid him. I'd say he wants the *Swan* badly. The jerk." He looked up from the chart of the Grenadine Islands and faced her, his eyes glittering with anticipation. "Now what?"

Leda was still trying to assimilate all the information he'd dumped on her. "Now what, what?"

"What comes after I've said I love you?" he asked calmly. "I've never said it to a woman before."

"You're kidding!"

163

"I'm not."

"But that's ridiculous! You were married!"

"It was a very sophisticated relationship."

"Didn't you promise to love, honor, cherish—"

"We wrote our own vows. Anne-Marie thought the word 'love' was overused. We made no mention of it. Leda, I meant what I said. I do love you. I think. But don't expect me to be fluent at saying so. My voice doesn't even sound natural to me. It sounds . . . surprised." He shook his head almost imperceptibly. "I don't know what the hell's going on. So now what?" he repeated.

Leda threw up her hands in a gesture of frustration. "How am I supposed to know? Do you think there's an authorized manual on how to fall in love properly? It's not as straightforward as an oil change, you know." This wasn't at all what she had imagined the moment would be. In fact, Nat was infuriating her with his confused candor. How could someone so incredibly romantic be so unromantic? "You're the man," she finished up peevishly. "You're supposed to know these things."

His grin was instant and broad. "That, from Ms. 'Anything-You-Can-Do-I-Can-Do-Better'? What about you? Where do a certain woman's feelings enter into all of this?" His look wavered between hopeful and sardonic.

"What a dumb question! Isn't it obvious that I've loved you practically since we met?" she challenged.

"You could've fooled *me*." He laughed, plopping into the navigator's seat and looking up at her with an ironic smile. His hands dangled between his outspread knees; tapping his fingertips together, he said, in his appealingly fake American accent, "Ain't love grand?"

He was too much for her. It was impossible, literally impossible, to stay angry with him. Sunshine brightness broke through Leda's frustration and she answered, "Ain't it, though?" and bent over to him, taking his bearded face between her hands and settling a sweet and deep, lingering kiss on his mouth. "I love you, Nat," she whispered.

164

"Captain . . . oh, Cap-tain!" The voice on deck was high-pitched with impatience.

"Good grief," Leda moaned. "Is she typical?"

"Worse than most," Nat shrugged. "Normally I'm able to screen charter clients; nearly all of my charters have been fun."

Leda slipped into the main cabin as Nat opened the hatch that led into the cockpit and said, "Yes, my fair Wilhelmina?"

"Call me Mina, Nathan." She giggled. "Do you suppose Leda could bring me a towel? I'd get one for myself, but I wouldn't want to track saltwater belowdecks," she explained with airy graciousness.

"Ah, but that's what boats are *for*, Mina," Nat said smoothly. "You just come down and track away to your heart's content."

"I'd rather she brought the towel up here."

"Anything you say, Meany. Ah, that's Min-*a*, isn't it?" he corrected himself innocently.

Leda, who heard the exchange, was on deck in seconds with a fresh, clean towel and a genuinely pleased smile on her face.

After the dishes were cleared, the duffel bags stowed, the anchor weighed, the sails raised, the course for Bequia set; after the course was sailed, the sails dropped, the sundowners served, and the salty boat hosed down; after dinner was cooked and dinner was cleared and all the dishes of the day washed and dried; after the Stevensons' beds were turned down and Tippy was run ashore for his fourth and hopefully last walk of the day; after, in short, a typical day in the grueling charter trade, Leda found herself alone in the tiny berth in the tiny forward cabin, her body and her mind limp with fatigue.

Even more than the cooking and serving, the fetching and the cleaning up, she found enforced conversation with Wilhelmina Stevenson exhausting. Leda now knew everything there was to know about breeding Scottish terriers. And how to win at contract bridge. And why today's children had such atrocious manners. She plumped her pillow mercilessly, pretending it was Wilhelmina Stevenson's hairdo, and was drifting off wearily to sleep when a soft hum on the intercom beside her berth announced that the aft cabin wished to communicate with the forward cabin.

"Leda? Are you asleep?" Nat's voice was soothingly quiet.

She held down the answer button. "Give me fifteen seconds and I will be," she said wearily.

"I just wanted to tell you that I think you make an outstanding crewmember."

"The charter isn't over yet, Captain," she demurred, pleased nonetheless. His voice was so near. . . .

"Leda, this arrangement is silly. Come back to my cabin," he said caressingly. "I've already conceded that you're a first-rate professional—what can you still be trying to prove?"

"Nothing, Nat. Let me think about it. I'll come to you if . . . if I can," she said vaguely. He'd laugh if she told him the real reason she'd insisted on sleeping in the crew's cabin: that, if she slept with him, they would surely make love; and she might, as she had last night, moan with pleasure, cry out with rapture. And two obnoxious strangers would overhear the sounds of their most intimate moments.

His voice acknowledged defeat. "Come if you can, then." Disappointment lingered in the air after the hum of the intercom went silent.

It was so stupid. Why should she give up a night of being held in Nat's arms just because of her puritanical modesty? Why be intimidated by a woman who treated her like Cinderella? *Stupid*. She decided to wait half an hour for the Stevensons to fall asleep; then she'd tiptoe up on deck and sneak aft, into Nat's cabin, into his arms.

CHAPTER ELEVEN

Staying awake for another half hour was about as likely as flying to the moon and back; Leda simply couldn't do it. Her eyelids drooped, then fell, then fluttered open; drooped again, fell, and this time, stayed closed. And when Leda's little quartz alarm clock *bip-bipped* her awake at six the next morning, she awoke with the feeling of emptiness that follows missed opportunity.

Slipping quietly into the galley, Leda began preparing breakfast. Ashore, Bequians were beginning to stir. Goats bleated, dogs barked, an islander's friendly voice called out a musical greeting. *Friendship Rose,* a local schooner that ferried between Bequia and St. Vincent every day, putt-putted past the *Swan,* the sounds of its ancient, wheezy engine splitting the sunny early-morning calm. Mixing a bowl of pancake batter, Leda told herself that this was what the Caribbean was all about: simple, charming pleasures like early-morning pancakes and piping hot coffee in the cockpit. A contradictory sigh escaped her. If only she could wave a wand over the Stevensons and turn them into, oh, her sister and her brother-in-law, for example. If only.

Leda was slicing into a thick slab of Canadian bacon when Nat dropped in—literally—through the hatch opening overhead. His face was so welcome. "Hi," she beamed. "I hope you're hungry."

"Starved," he said wryly, taking her in his arms and kissing her. "I suppose," he whispered, nibbling on her lower lip, "that you slept disgustingly well?"

Automatically her arms had slid around his neck; she stood

back slightly, captivated as always by the deeply tanned and bearded face with its intensely blue eyes as he stood, awash in sunlight, below the open hatch. "I slept very well, I'm sorry to say," she said with an apologetic smile.

"God, I can't stand it," he objected good-humoredly. "You eat like a draft horse, sleep like a top . . . so healthy. And so eminently sane."

"It's the clean living that does it," she murmured, sticking out her pink, healthy tongue and flicking it over his with a light, teasing motion. She felt sinfully flirtatious this morning.

"Careful, little sea witch," he threatened huskily, "don't start anything you can't finish." His mouth engulfed hers as his arms held her tightly. "Leda . . . dope . . . why didn't you stay with me last night?" he whispered.

"You'd laugh if I told you," she answered, curving her neck like a cat beneath his caress.

"You'd feel shy in front of the company?" he asked.

"Well, yes. How did you know?"

"Just psychic, I guess." He chuckled. "Not to mention, you nearly pushed me overboard when I put my arm around you on the foredeck yesterday evening."

"You haven't seen the letters that I have, from charterers complaining about promiscuous captains and their crew. Why do you think I fantasized so easily about Juanita and you?" she confessed, averting her head and pouring out a ladle of batter onto the griddle.

"Surely you know by now that I'm a one-woman man," he said softly, sticking the tip of his index finger in the batter and licking it. "How about adding some blueberries to this?"

"Nat," Leda began slowly, determined not to let the conversation stray this time, "if you're a one-woman man, why don't you do something about it?" She arranged the limp slabs of bacon carefully in the pan, acting thoroughly engrossed in her task.

"Do something . . . such as what?" he asked quietly.

"Such as"—she stole a look at his attentive, serious face—

"such as a proposal of some sort or other. It needn't be of marriage, you know."

For a long moment he said nothing, staring, with Leda, at the bacon as it became soft, then transparent, then began to sizzle. At last he said simply, "But you're the marrying kind."

"And you're not? Ever again?" She turned to him to hear his answer with her undivided attention, a sense of sickening déjà vu pervading her. Was she doomed to go through her final scene with Jeffrey all over again?

"I don't know; I just don't know," he admitted. "Leda, I'm no Victorian hero. I'm not about to ask you to wait a couple of years for me."

"Wait . . . for what?" she asked blankly, suddenly realizing that her first batch of pancakes had burned on one side. Hastily she scraped them into the waste can, then put the empty griddle back on the open flame. "I mean, it's not as though you're waiting to finish medical school, or to complete an apprenticeship in jewelry-making," she argued. She hated herself for pushing; where was her pride? "Wait for what?" she repeated.

"Wait for me to—you know—sail around the world. God, it sounds so idiotically pompous. How can I make you understand that it's a dream as old as you are? I owe it to myself, to my parents. If I married you, if I gave the idea up—a third time —I'd never be at peace with myself. I don't expect you to understand," he said gently, tiredly.

"Is *that* all?" she asked, ecstatically relieved at the progress she'd made. "Take me with you, Nat. I want desperately to go."

"Ah, there's the rub. I can't. I tried it once. I can't. Anne-Marie—"

"Anne-Marie has nothing to do with me," she said, suddenly angry. "I'm strong, able, I don't get—stay—sick. My God, how many more tests do I have to pass before I qualify?" Her voice rose in frustration.

"You're as nearly perfect as can be," he said, lifting a loose strand of hair and tucking it back into her single braid. "But you're a woman," he added doggedly, his voice filled with a strange and touching sadness.

169

"So what?" she shouted in exasperation.

"So what if you should become pregnant?"

Exasperated, she said, "Being pregnant isn't an eternal condition, you know; eventually a baby *is* born, you know."

A look of sudden, intense pain crossed his face. "Not always," he said softly.

Leda looked at him, puzzled, and then burst into a fit of tearful coughing; the griddle, left untended and empty over the high flame, had overheated, filling the galley with pungent smoke. Nat had been as oblivious to it as she. Leda grabbed the handle, forgetting to use a potholder, and promptly burned the palm of her hand. Dropping the pan with a sudden gasp of pain, she stood wincing and teary-eyed, but whether the tears were of smoke or pain or frustration, she didn't know.

Nat turned the palm of her hand over gently. "Ouch. That'll burn for a bit. Run it under cold water, quickly." And he led her hand, with Leda trailing along behind it, to the galley sink. At that moment a head appeared, upside down, in the hatch opening overhead.

"Don't burn the damn boat down before I've had a chance to buy it," Stevenson grumbled. "Where's that winch handle, Nat?"

"Oh, for God's . . . I'd forgotten, Mark. I'll bring it up; in the meantime, why don't you start the engine?" As Mark withdrew, Nat said to Leda apologetically, "I'm not being very attentive either to you or my charter party, am I? That hand doesn't look too bad; think you can manage breakfast while we're under way? Mark wants to go directly to Tobago Cays in time for a late lunch." He blew gently on the burn. "Let me put some salve on that."

"Don't be silly, it doesn't hurt at all," she lied. "Go on with whatever you were doing. Do you need help with the anchor?"

"Mark wants to do it. What the hell, it's his back." Nat grinned. "Yell if you need help down here," he said, dropping a feathery kiss just beside the pink burn mark.

After a brief delay—for Tippy's first walk ashore of the day —the *Swan* was off and sailing in the light morning breeze.

Pancakes were more easily made in a harbor than on the ocean, Leda found. In theory, the stove was designed to swing on gimbals to compensate for the motion of the boat. In practice, things didn't work out quite that way. The batter on the griddle oozed to starboard when the boat swayed to port, and vice-versa. An extra-large pancake crept over the edge of the griddle, drooling down into the burners; like all the other pancakes, it was oblong-shaped. Next time, she'd cook oatmeal.

After breakfast, Wilhelmina returned to her berth, feeling queasy, and Leda was free to perch up in the bow, reveling in the crystalline beauty of the waters around the Tobago Cays. Every conceivable shade and variation of blue could be found here, from aquamarine shoals to sapphire depths. The Cays themselves, a cluster of tiny, uninhabited islands, were protected from the huge rollers of the Atlantic Ocean by Horseshoe Reef, an aptly named coral barrier to the east and upwind of the islands. It was another side of the Caribbean, elemental, wild, overwhelmingly beautiful.

Despite Leda's burn, despite the mess in the galley, despite her confusion over Nat's stubborn refusal to take her with him, the afternoon turned out to be a memorably happy one, mostly because Wilhelmina had a bad case of cabin fever and wanted desperately to spend some time ashore. The Stevensons, two lounge chairs, an overflowing picnic basket, a beach umbrella—and Tippy—were deposited on a little spit of white sand on Baradal Island, and Nat and Leda were alone on the *Swan.*

"Well, darlin'," Nat suggested, "we can clean up the mess below, or we can go snorkeling. Which?"

"Which do you think?" she answered, delighted. "Wait'll I grab my suit."

Ah, the suit. Leda slipped into the new red bikini, which had got much smaller, much brighter, than when she'd tried it on in the boutique. She threw a blue terry-cloth cover-up over her mostly naked body and scampered out to the skiff, where Nat waited for her, the picture of impatience. "Food!" she cried. "I forgot food! I'll be right back."

"Hold it!" He waved a small duffel at her. "A loaf of bread

and a jug of wine. And thou, naturally. Or is it 'thee'?" he wondered dispassionately. "Jump in."

They tore off for the last snippets of land on the western Atlantic, World's End Reef. The outboard engine, running full-out, was deafening, and they said little until they found themselves among the mostly submerged, partly awash reefs. Maneuvering the skiff carefully among the browns and golds of the reefs, Nat at length tossed a grapnel over the side to anchor the skiff, and dragged out two sets of masks and flippers.

"Lady, you're about to dip into the eighth wonder of the world." He came aft with her gear as Leda, with illogical shyness, pulled her cover-up over her head, feeling very much like a mermaid on a rock in the middle of the ocean.

"Oh, my dear, sweet creature. Where, oh where, did you get that suit?" he said, his voice low with elemental appreciation.

"A locally made product," she answered lightly. "Do you like it?"

"I do. Why haven't you worn it before now?"

"Wilhelmina hates the color red, remember?" Really, his smoldering look was almost too hot to bear; she picked up her mask and began adjusting the band around her head.

"No, wait. I . . . Leda, there isn't another living soul for miles. Take off your suit; I'll take off mine. We owe this to ourselves. It feels surprisingly . . . different, to snorkel without clothing," he promised.

"Huh! And I thought you liked the suit," she teased, reaching behind her to untie the back string.

"Your suit," he said, slipping off his black nylon briefs, "did what it was supposed to do—got itself removed as quickly as possible."

She was undressed now, and feeling a little comical as she pulled a pair of black rubber flippers over her feet.

"Leda," Nat began in a low, suggestive voice, "the reef will still be there tomorrow. . . ."

Her turn now; she surveyed his muscled form with calculated innocence. "Have you lured me out here on false pretenses, Captain? I thought the eighth wonder of the world," she said, pointing to the reef below them, "was supposed to be down *there*."

To her astonishment, Nat colored perceptibly. "All right, all right. Snorkeling it is, then."

Leda eased herself, after Nat, over the side of the skiff, adjusted her mask and snorkel tube, and set out to explore the underworld paradise that lurked beneath her.

It was a case, very simply, of sensory overload. Dazzling, awesome beauty stretched out below her in startling clarity as far as she could see. Intricate coral formations—fan coral, star coral, brain coral, corals she'd never seen before—were house and home to hundreds of gaudy-colored fish, all eager to outdazzle their neighbors. Yellow and black angelfish a foot high swam serenely among fat, fleshy parrotfish, green and bright and comically mean-looking. Leda spotted yellowjack, red snapper and a ballooned-out pufferfish, poisonous to eat but not dangerous otherwise.

Out of the corner of her mask she was aware of Nat swimming close by, a comforting thought. Things were very, very exotic down here, and even though Leda hovered on the water's surface, she was aware that she was *not* a mermaid, and water was not her native element. She turned and made a sudden, startled movement as a small squid darted under her belly. Everywhere the reef teemed with movement and sea life. Nat swam a little ahead, then turned to face her, mask to mask, and pointed to a small sand shark, harmless and lazy, basking nearby. Well, well. Perhaps it was time for a little break.

She motioned to Nat to return with her to the skiff and she led the way, feeling simultaneously enveloped and exposed by the warm, transparent water. As they neared the skiff, Nat took over the lead; it was Leda's chance to savor the poetry of his muscled, capable form gliding ahead and alongside of her. He was right out of Jacques Cousteau—minus half a yard of cloth, of course.

"Well," he said, tossing her a beach towel when they were back in the skiff, "what did you think?"

"Spooky. Eerie. Sensational. I'd like to do it again. Someday,

173

in fact," she continued, rubbing her hair cursorily with the towel before wrapping it around her body, "I'd like to learn how to use scuba gear. This was fine but . . . too tantalizing. I wanted more," she admitted.

"I know *just* what you mean," he grinned, plopping himself and his food bag beside her in the anchored skiff. Suddenly he asked, "Have you ever made love in the ocean?"

"Uh . . . no, can't say that I have. Is that *cheese?*" Leda's stomach began growling emptily, right on cue.

"We'll have to try it sometime," he announced serenely. Slicing off a hunk of cheese and then a slab of bread with his jackknife, he asked, "A skiff? Ever made love in a skiff?"

"Nope. You've got me there again, I'm afraid."

He held the cheese a little above her head. "Would you like lunch before . . . or after?" he asked, his face dancing with humor.

Leda eyed the slab of cheese; eyed Nat's increasingly interested form; thoughtfully bit her lower lip, considering; and said, "After."

That night, under a rare starless sky, the wind moaned continuously and wretchedly through the rigging of the *Swan.* After the bright, brief, loving afternoon of fantasy and escape, the sound seemed unbearably ominous to Leda, lying alone in the forward cabin. She cursed herself for deciding, again, to sleep apart from Nat. Rolling over onto her stomach in the cramped berth, covering her ears with her pillow, Leda tried to will herself into a state of thoughtlessness.

The boat, protected by Horseshoe Reef from the rolling Atlantic, hardly moved. But with no hills or mountains to hide behind, the *Swan* stood utterly exposed, like a lone horse in a vast moor on a black night, waiting for the dawn. Leda pressed the pillow down tightly over her ears. The wind! The constant, sinister, peace-shattering wind! How would she bear the sound for four more hours of darkness? The wind whistled, it whined, it clawed at the awning, a bodiless ghost, threatening nameless violence.

A wire halyard had been left slack inadvertently; it rapped against the tall, aluminum mast with peevish monotony. Leda would never be able to fall asleep until she went up on deck and tied it away from the mast.

She slid open the hatch above her berth and climbed up onto the foredeck, instantly chilled and dampened by the night. The light cotton shift she wore whipped around her knees as she secured the offending wire, and she was about to dash back below, before the low-scudding rain clouds in the east overtook her, when she saw the dark figure hurry forward from the cockpit.

"Leda! You tied off that goddamned halyard, then?" Nat's voice was tense and low as he put his arm around her and propelled her back toward the cockpit. "Come below; it's going to pour in another minute."

Nat had barely slid the hatch to his cabin shut when the squall hit. With shocking fury it slapped the *Swan* over on its side; the boat heeled, as if it were at sea, then righted itself; and then the rain fell. Buckets, torrents, a wall of rain. Leda and Nat stared out the portholes at . . . nothing. At drenching wetness.

"I'm glad I let out some extra chain before I turned in; the anchor seems to have held," Nat said tiredly. He took Leda's cold hands in his, rubbing them briskly. "Get into bed, you're chilled through."

"All right," she whispered, climbing into the double berth, "but can you speak more quietly?" She pulled the light blanket over her shoulders, trying not to shiver.

"The Stevensons can't possibly understand what we're saying," he reassured her in a normal voice.

"If you say so," she answered, dropping her voice still further.

Nat climbed into bed alongside her, fitting his body to the curve of hers, passing on as much warmth as he could. "Better?"

Leda burrowed more deeply into his warmth; the shiver, when it came, was of relieved contentment. Outside, the thundering rain stopped as abruptly as it began, and the wind resumed its low, dreary moan.

After a bit, Nat changed position and lay on his back, drawing Leda onto his chest, enveloping her with his secure sailor's hold. "I hate a night like this," he confessed.

"You too? Why?" she asked, surprised. With her, the reason was simple, irrational fear. But Nat?

"Who knows?" he said, absently stroking her hair. "I suppose I worry about the anchor dragging. I suppose I remember . . . Anne-Marie. Our last night at sea together was wild and squally, like this." He exhaled suddenly, as if a secret were being dragged from him by force. "We turned back to England on a night like this. She was so frightened. I never, never should have tried to make her go on," he admitted, his voice husky with remorse.

Leda lay curled on his chest without stirring, almost without breathing. Nat was teetering, she felt, on the brink of something. Of pouring out something to her at last. She phrased her words slowly, cautiously, as she would to a sleepwalker, careful not to startle him. "But you didn't make Anne-Marie do anything, Nat. You *did* turn the boat around. What more could you have done?"

"I could have turned around twenty-four hours earlier, and Anne-Marie wouldn't have lost the . . . had the . . . miscarriage." His voice was flat, exhausted, without emotion.

For a moment Leda said nothing. Then: "Anne-Marie was pregnant?" Suddenly all the pieces began falling into place for Leda: Nat's chronic secretiveness; his fierce attempt to remain emotionally aloof; his agonized refusal to let Leda share his sailing dream.

"She was three months pregnant. I didn't know, of course— we made love so rarely—but probably I wouldn't have considered it a problem if I *had* known. I didn't know much about those things then."

It all seemed a bit melodramatic to Leda; surely modern couples confided such matters to one another. "She never told you she was pregnant before . . . . ?"

176

"Nope. We had agreed she'd be on the pill for a while. Apparently she forgot to take a couple of them—I think when her purse was stolen—and then, by the time she discovered she was pregnant, we were well into the preparations for our circumnavigation."

"She must have wanted to go with you very much," Leda admitted, oddly distressed by Anne-Marie's devotion.

"Oh, no, she made that very clear after the . . . the thing happened. It was just that she was very stubborn, very proud. Very sure she could handle it. In some ways she reminds me of you," he said softly, his hand lying still on her golden hair.

Leda raised herself up on one elbow and looked at him with wide eyes. "I'd never, *never* keep a thing like that from you! Anyway, you would know," she added, thinking of how much, how often, how desperately she wanted him. How would he not know?

"Shh, you're nothing like Anne-Marie, darling, really. She had the spirit, but not your follow-through." He laughed a short, bitter laugh. "And I'm pretty sure you'd never throw the thing in my face the way she did. God, it was such a nightmare: the weather; her panic; the decision to turn around. And then the revelation, after it was too late. And after that, her endless recriminations, all the way back to England. And the worst of it was, it really was my fault; I never should've taken on the responsibilities of marriage. Not then. Not now. You see?" he whispered into her hair.

"Ah, poor Nat. I understand. I do understand what you're saying," she said, her voice low with compassion. Her arm slid around his neck as she pressed herself close to him, reassuring him. He was entirely wrong about himself, she knew, but now was not the time to try to convince him. Now he needed comfort, and love, and to know that she, at least, would not reproach him.

"I've never told anyone before," he said quietly. "I'm sure Anne-Marie has by now, but I . . . couldn't. It never seemed like anyone's business, and I just couldn't."

"Sometimes, you need to share," she said, remembering the

177

sense of relief she'd felt after confiding to him her hurt and anger over Jeffrey. Just saying the thing outright had made it all less significant to her; would it be that way for Nat? She marveled at the depth of his guilt. After all, if he didn't even *know* . . .

And yet, the experience must have been burned deeply into his consciousness. It wasn't hard for Leda, listening to the incessant whine of the wind, to imagine what it must have been like on an eerie, squally night, a hundred miles at sea, fighting seasickness, bracing everywhere against the boat's wild motion, tired and inexperienced and frightened. How tragically dumb of Anne-Marie not to have told Nat sooner—Nat, the best possible ally a woman could want. What a waste. And what an appalling shock for Nat. Leda closed her eyes, dismissing the painful scene from her mind. Anne-Marie's behavior seemed incomprehensible to her; Nat's wife was too sophisticated, her motives too indecipherable for Leda's sensible, practical mind.

Nat had drifted into a deep, sound sleep, and Leda lay curled against his chest, listening to his steady breathing and to the wind moaning in the rigging.

CHAPTER TWELVE

Nat had been gone for weeks. It was May, and now Leda was leaving Bequia too. A sign overhead flashed FASTEN SEAT BELTS, and in minutes Leda was lifted up and away, bound for Boston. Good-bye to Paradise. Without Nat, it wasn't Paradise any longer; it was only unbearably and hellishly hot. The charter season had all but ended. Restaurants were closing for the Caribbean summer; guesthouses emptying; yachts deserting the island in droves for fashionable harbors up north. There was nothing for a dejected workaholic to do but to remember.

To remember, line for line and word for word, the last, heartbreaking conversation she'd had with Nat the night before he sailed from Bequia, headed for Florida to deliver the *Swan.* The boat had been sold, of course; it was perfect for the Stevensons. Leda had sliced and diced, sautéed and souffléed her way into a good impression, and had helped to make the sale a reality. How ironic; if she hadn't been so good at what she did, maybe the *Swan* wouldn't have been sold and Nat would have stayed on in Bequia, aimless and undecided about what to do with his life. But no; instead he was selling the *Swan,* buying a smaller boat, and setting off at last on his dream cruise.

Leda gazed absently out the window of the 727 jet at the vast blue ocean, at the color of sapphire eyes. She looked away, shut her eyes, prayed for night to fall. It was, so far, her worst moment—this breaking with their shared, common experience. Tomorrow Leda would be back in Newport, at her old job; she needed desperately the distraction of hard work. She wondered whether Nat would ever read her deliberately lighthearted postcard, sent to London, to his only permanent address: "Had all the fun I can stand; think I'll head back to Newport and the work ethic."

She bit her lower lip, uncertain whether to cry or to rail at fate. He was so frustrating. Stubborn. *Immovable.* Leda had pulled out every argument in her debater's bag that last sunset together in Admiralty Bay.

"I'd be on the pill," she'd pointed out logically.

"That's what Anne-Marie said. Women change their minds all the time," he'd insisted.

"Let's say we did change our minds about having a baby; then we'd stop somewhere and stay there until the baby was born," she had argued.

"Oh, sure, in some outpost in the Pacific?"

"Babies are born in the Pacific every day, Nat. And what about Singapore? What about your mother, for Pete's sake?"

"My mother was lucky, just lucky. She was taking a terrible risk having me," he'd answered.

"Damn it, Nat, driving on an expressway is a terrible risk. I don't want to spend the rest of my life safe and sound in a clothes closet. Will you take me with you, or not?"

"No. I love you. No."

That had been his answer. And that had been when Leda blew up all her bridges in one glorious, stupid stroke. "Fine. Don't. But don't expect me to sit around waiting for your next postcard. Because I don't want to know that you're having a wonderful time and wish I was there. I won't wait for you, Nat. I won't."

He had answered with infinite, loving tenderness, "Darling, don't you think I know that?" And except for a cable addressed impersonally to Coco's Chartering Service announcing that the *Swan* had arrived safely in Fort Lauderdale, Leda had heard nothing further from him. So much for ultimatums.

Drinks were being served by the airline stewardess, and Leda ordered and paid for a rum and cola. She unscrewed the cap to the tiny bottle of rum and instantly became overwhelmed by a tumble of associations. Rum punches at the jump-up at the Sunny Caribe. Rum flips on the *Swan* during that wonderful, exhausting week. Piña coladas in the cockpit, during their last sunset together. She corked the little bottle back up, locking the genie of sweet memory away, and sipped her cola straight.

When it came right down to it, she thought drearily, what did she know, really, about men's dreams of adventure? Maybe men were motivated differently than women. Marco Polo, Magellan, Columbus . . . She wondered which of them was married, what they told their wives. If Mrs. Polo had put her foot down, could she have gone along too? Probably not. *Oh, the hell with it.* Leda had done what she could, and it wasn't enough. She had to get on, somehow, with what was left of her life. Maybe she could shuttle back and forth between Bequia and Newport forever, alternately running from and reliving the winter's dream.

Spring in Newport meant two things: fog, and the sound of hammering. It was the fifth straight day of a northeast wind, the fifth straight day of damp, thick fog; Leda's tan was fading fast. At the same time, it *was* spring, and developers were doing their frenzied best to cram more shops, more boutiques, more condominiums into what little space was left on the Newport waterfront. From her second-floor office overlooking the harbor, Leda stared with loathing at a rapidly rising building under construction close by; it would ruin her view to the south. And the view of the harbor, for some unlucky townspeople. *And* the view of the quaint City-by-the-Sea, for a lot of anchored yachtsmen. She had assumed that the condominium would stop at two stories, but this morning she'd noticed framework going up for a third. Nuts. In another month the rays of the sun wouldn't be able to filter into her old-fashioned, cluttered, refreshingly unrestored office. The hammers pounded endlessly next door. Leda lifted her mug of morning tea in a solitary, ironic toast: *Here's to progress, fellas.*

In the last week Leda had settled so effortlessly into her old Newport routine that she began to feel as though the months in Bequia had been a little fantasy she'd spun to warm her through the long New England winter. She pulled her navy lambswool sweater back on over her head; it was obvious that the fog was not going to burn off this morning. It was hard to believe that somewhere behind that thick, impenetrable pea soup was a bright, warm sun. The harbor, in fact, had disappeared entirely again. The wind had died away, and big, lazy raindrops splatted on the roof of her low-ceilinged office. From the main channel of fogbound Narragansett Bay came the ominous sound of a freighter's foghorn, warning smaller vessels to move out of the way. The circulating siren on the Newport Bridge cut through the thick fog with its high, shrill cry, announcing, to those who cared, that it would not move out of anyone's way.

Spring in Newport: not especially sunny, and rarely ever hot; but it had a melancholy charm of its own. At least she wasn't feeling sorry, as she had in Bequia, for having to work indoors. Who'd want to be outside—or worse, on a boat—on a day like this? Take that poor yacht circling around the fuel dock. . . .

"My God," she said aloud, "it's the *Swan.*"

Or was it? Leda thought she'd recognized the high, distinctive bow of the yacht, poking its nose through the fog, but before she'd made a positive identification, it was gone again, swallowed whole. She pressed her nose against the multipaned window, straining to see if the yacht would return, her whole body throbbing from the shock of recognition. It had to be the *Swan;* no other boat had a bow like that.

Grabbing her bright-green hooded rain jacket, Leda ran blindly down the narrow, ramshackle hallway, stumbling on the bottom step, brushing past her open-mouthed boss, who was on his way upstairs with a bag of doughnuts; running like a madwoman down Thames Street to the shipyard, where the boat seemed about to dock; not stopping until she spied the *Swan*—it was the *Swan*—tied up at the end of the pier.

Then, only then, she paused, caught her breath, and rehearsed a quick little introductory speech for the Stevensons: *Hello, how are you, I couldn't care less, where's Nat?* Well, something to that effect, anyway. Jamming her fists deep into her pockets, her hood pulled up to keep her damp hair from getting

182

any damper, Leda sauntered deliberately, like a tourist on a sunny day, down to the end of the dock.

A tall blond young man wearing yellow foul-weather gear was adjusting a dock line from the foredeck of the *Swan*. She didn't recognize him from Bequia; the Stevensons must have hired someone of their own as crew. A feeling intensely proprietary swept over Leda. This stranger had no business on her lovely *Swan;* she wanted to yank him off the boat and throw him in the harbor. He was acting like such hot stuff, putting on airs. What did he know of the incredible days and nights she'd spent aboard the *Swan?*

It was impossible to overcome the hostility she felt for the unsuspecting usurper. Leda walked past him, toward the cockpit aft, and only then noticed the yellow quarantine flag flying from the starboard spreader. Funny; why would the Stevensons be flying a Q-flag if they'd just sailed up from Florida? Unless they came via Bermuda?

The man in the cockpit, dressed and hooded in orange foul-weather gear, stood with his back to Leda, coiling a jibsheet. It certainly was not pudgy Mark Stevenson.

"Nat!" she half wailed, refusing, still, to believe in fairy tales.

"Leda!" His voice sounded nearly as surprised as hers as he spun around at her cry.

Her foot was on the boarding ladder at the gate. "No, don't come aboard!" he said quickly.

Surprised, she backed away hastily and stood on the dock. "Why?" she bantered uncertainly. "Does someone aboard have yellow fever?"

The familiar look of sardonic humor settled on his Roman brow as he walked forward on the deck to just opposite where she stood on the dock. "No, you darling ninny; but Customs hasn't cleared us yet. Since I'm not a U.S. citizen, I think I'd better go by the book. He'll be here any minute," he added apologetically, sweeping over her face and form with an intense, almost fierce look.

Dropping to a sitting position on deck, his legs slung over the side of the hull, his arms resting on the lifelines, he met her gaze at eye level. Crystal droplets of fog clung to his beard, his eyebrows, his mustache. He'd thrown back his hood, and his black hair, rain-soaked, clung to his neck and brow in unkempt curls. She'd never seen anyone so handsome in her life.

"For a landlubber, you move around a lot, lady," he said reproachfully.

"*I* move around! Where have *you* been?" she asked, pointing up at the Q-flag. "And where are the Stevensons?" And why wouldn't her heart stop hammering?

"The Stevensons," he said dryly, "found themselves 'financially encumbered,' as Mark put it; the sale fell through. I'd done a lot of soul-searching by then, anyway, and decided to sail back to Bequia—and to you. You, however, had fled the island by the time I returned."

"Why didn't you call, for heaven's sake!" Her hands had moved unconsciously, lovingly, illegally, to his; he held them tightly in his grasp.

"I did call; the overseas lines to St. Vincent and Bequia were down for a couple of days, remember? Anyway, why didn't *you* write that you were leaving Bequia?"

"I did, to London. Lord—and they call this the age of instant communication!" she laughed giddily.

"Partly it was my imbecilic desire to surprise you," he confessed. "And then when I finally landed at Bequia, and Julie said you'd left the island, I remember just sitting at your desk, stunned. I considered flying back up, but that'd leave the *Swan* untended, and I wanted it where we'd be, anyway."

"And the phone lines were down again?" she asked with wry amusement.

"I was afraid you'd ask that. No, the reason I didn't call you from Bequia was that I didn't want to explain being too stupid to have called in the first place. Does that make sense to anyone but me?" he asked ingenuously.

"Nope, but who's complaining?" she teased.

"So I sailed straight back to Newport," he continued breathlessly, "a rotten, slow trip, head winds the last few days, rain . . . and as for that Cro-Magnon on the bow . . ." he said, dropping his voice and nodding toward the burly crewmember. "Desperate; I was desperate, or I wouldn't have taken him . . . has to be told everything—"

"I thought that's the way you liked it, Captain," she said with malicious glee.

"Not since you crewed for me; I just never could trust anyone before. I had to find everything for him. Which, of course, I couldn't, since you'd moved it all around—always, damn you, to a more logical place. How any woman could make herself so indispensable in one short week . . . Where's the chili sauce, by the way?"

"Um, with the canned tomato products, in the outboard bin on the port side of the galley."

"See? Makes more sense than with soy sauce, which is where I kept it. Leda," he said suddenly, seriously, "I was so . . . lost without you. So sure you'd be in Bequia, waiting. It was the most devastating moment of my life when I walked into Coco's and found you'd gone. I can't live like that."

A small motor scooter putt-putted up to the end of the dock, and a uniformed customs agent dismounted. Leda jumped away guiltily from Nat, freeing her hands from his grip. The agent, an extremely kind-looking man whose gray mustache all but hid his quiet, friendly smile, introduced himself and said, "I hope you had a good trip, Captain?"

Shaking his hand, Nat answered, "I've had worse, sir," and the two went below, with the Cro-Magnon, to complete the necessary paperwork.

Leda paced impatiently up and down the dock, delirious with joy, drinking in the details of the *Swan,* remembering a dozen different moments of happy intimacy: cocktails on the bow; watching for a "green flash" in the Caribbean sunset; an uproarious tickling match on the sole of the cockpit; diving into crystal water from the lower spreaders of the mast, twenty-five feet above the water. Wait. Something was different. The mast, the lower spreaders. Gone! There were two masts now, each smaller than the old, tall, single one. Smaller sails, smaller everything. Why on earth did Nat re-rig the *Swan* from a sloop to a ketch?

In minutes the friendly customs agent was disembarking; and behind him, the blond usurper, with his duffel bag. Pumping Nat's large hand with his even larger one, the crewman said, "Hey, man. Good trip."

"Piece o' cake," Nat agreed with a wry smile.

"Look me up if you need crew again," the blond giant insisted earnestly.

"Who else?" Nat watched the massive figure lumber away from the *Swan,* then turned to Leda with a friendly grimace. "There he goes, the original Incredible Hulk. He was nearly washed overboard a couple of times; thank God he was wearing a safety harness, or I wouldn't have cleared Customs nearly so easily," he said, laughing.

Suddenly she remembered to worry for Nat's safety. "Nat! Was it a rough trip, then?"

"Piece o' cake," he repeated, looking pleased with himself for the Americanism. "The man has no sense of balance, that's all; it turned out he has an inner ear problem. Personally, I think he's missing his inner ears altogether; he didn't seem to understand a thing I told him. Leda," Nat said, holding his arms out to her as she stood on the dock, "you've ruined me forever. Welcome aboard, darlin'," he added softly.

They were the sweetest words she'd ever heard. In two leaps she was on the ladder and in his arms, being lifted, hugged, kissed, as she never had before.

"Ah, Leda, I was such a jerk. Such a *fool,* such a jerk. In Florida it dawned on me, finally, that I'd been stalling those years in the Caribbean, waiting for the right and perfect mate. Then you came along: right, perfect—and I loved you too much to endanger you. It was an absurd dilemma," he murmured, kissing away a dewdrop of fog that had fallen on her damp, flushed cheek. "Let's go down below."

"What let you finally resolve it?" she asked curiously, following him down the steps into his dearly familiar cabin, hanging up her wet rain jacket next to his.

"I realized—am I rationalizing?—that you can make your own decisions. I also realized that the *Swan* could be made safer for us both."

"Is that why you re-rigged the *Swan* to a ketch? Of course it is," she answered herself.

"Right. You're looking at a retired speed demon. Slow but sure is my new motto." Then, with an impish look he said, "But wait! There's more!" and threw open the door between his quarters and the main cabin.

Leda blinked in astonishment. "What happened to the old Passion Pit?"

"It's been made more suitable for family living." He smiled.

The cold, impersonal look had disappeared. Chrome, acrylic doors, black Naugahyde—all gone. The huge bar—gone, replaced by a small leaded-glass wine cabinet. Now there were rich red cushions; walnut-paneled bulkheads; an exquisite brass fireplace surrounded by antique delft tiles; and bookshelves, bookshelves everywhere.

"I don't believe it," she breathed. "Did you take notes?"

"Whenever you'd make a suggestion? Hardly, but I guess it all sank in, anyway."

"But . . . but when could you have had it all done?" she blurted.

"Six men, double shifts. Piece o' cake."

She was aware that he was watching her every move, reveling in her obvious appreciation of the miracle he'd wrought.

A tiny fire crackled in the fireplace, just the right size to dispel the chill of the Newport fog. "I love the fireplace, the fire. And new artwork too?" she asked, moving closer to examine a small, exquisitely framed oil painting tucked in a quiet corner of the cabin. It was a gracefully rendered version of a mythological scene, one which Leda recognized instantly: the seduction of Leda, her namesake, by Zeus in the form of a swan. She stared a long moment at the compelling, dramatic scene: at the golden-haired queen, her face partly averted, her long hair obscuring her cheek; at the great, powerful bird, his enormous white wing covering her body. It was suggestive, mysterious, alluring.

187

"Where did this come from?" she asked quietly, moved by feelings she couldn't possibly define.

"I had it commissioned. I know it's not a Rembrandt," he said quickly, "but I've always been so struck by the coincidence of the names—yours and the boat's. Even before I met you, when I saw your name on the job application, I made the connection. Sailors are superstitious, Leda; I'm afraid I'm as bad as all the rest." His expression was touchingly apologetic.

Visibly shaken, Leda walked up to Nat, slid her arms around his waist, and laid her head silently on his chest. More than anything else—more than the sight of the *Swan* in Newport; more than the fact of Nat's sailing to Bequia and back for her; more than his redesigning the interior of the *Swan* to satisfy her pleasure—the painting had stirred her soul.

"Ah, darling, you don't like it," he murmured into her hair, encircling her with his arms and rocking her back and forth gently.

"I do, Nat. Very much," she whispered.

"Do you?" he asked, relieved and pleased. "The painting is the reason I missed you in Bequia, you know. The fellow kept saying one more day, one more day. You can't rush an artist, of course; though how it can take so long to paint a piece of canvas nine by twelve inches. Leda . . . Leda, I love you so much," he said suddenly, his voice catching in his throat, his lips searching for hers, finding them, bruising them with aching love. It was a novel, sweet New England embrace: all woolly sweaters and blue jeans, wool slacks and warm socks. So many illusions and misunderstandings had dropped away between them. All that remained now were layers and layers of clothing.

"Nat . . . love me," she said in a low cry, overwhelmed with longing and love for him.

"Yes, Leda . . . yes," he answered hoarsely, lowering her gently to the deep-piled Oriental rug beneath them, undressing her in the glowing warmth of the fireplace with a tenderness that was almost painful to experience.

For her the act of loving him was a kaleidoscope of passion; each time, it was different. The colors, the shapes, the shimmer-

188

ing pinpoints of light inside her soul, were different each time he kissed her, thrilled her with his tongue, cherished her with his sailor's calloused loving hands.

It was with a sense of awe, of wonder, at the depth of her love for him, and his for her, that she accepted him, drew him into her, a woman incomplete, needing a man incomplete, to make a rapturous, ecstatic whole. She loved him so much.

Afterward they lay perfectly still in one another's arms in the fog-enshrouded cabin, their heads cradled in a nest of musky woolen sweaters, their bodies—at least, the upper part of their bodies—kept warm from the dying heat of the little brass fireplace. Then Nat slipped his arm out from underneath Leda, rolled over, and lifted the little screen from the fireplace, tossing half a dozen pieces of coal onto the grate. "I didn't know it could be . . . like that," he said softly.

"Like what?" she answered mistily.

He turned back to face her, propping his cheek on one hand, his other hand tracing the line of her eyebrow, the curve of her ear, gently affirming the reality of her. "I felt such yearning, for you. I didn't think it could possibly be satisfied."

"And was it?" she smiled, stretching luxuriously and bringing her hands behind her head, elbows out to the side. She felt as warm and cozy as a cat, happy, relaxed; for the first time since the awkward moment she'd first laid eyes on him, Leda felt completely, utterly free of tension. The future was theirs, theirs, theirs. *"Were* you satisfied?" she asked unnecessarily.

"Does McDonald's have arches?" He grinned. "Leda," he said more seriously, "there's one thing. Rightly or wrongly, I'm convinced you think I háte children."

"Wrongly." With his capacity for love? How silly of him.

"Because, as a matter of fact, I think we'll have to start thinking about raising a crew; why should *we* do all the work?" He chuckled, bending over to drop a light kiss on her shoulder.

She looked up at him quickly, her eyes shining with love and good humor. "It's certainly a thought. Do you suppose we could tear out that berth in the crew's cabin and put in a gimballed bassinet?"

"Piece o' cake," he said, lowering his mouth gently to hers.

LOOK FOR NEXT MONTH'S
CANDLELIGHT ECSTASY ROMANCES®

Candlelight

Ecstasy Romances™

$1.95 each

At your local bookstore or use this handy coupon for ordering:

DELL BOOKS
P.O. BOX 1000. PINE BROOK. N.J. 07058-1000   B187A

Please send me the books I have checked above. I am enclosing $_____ (please add 75c per copy to cover postage and handling). Send check or money order—no cash or C.O.D.'s. Please allow up to 8 weeks for shipment.

Name _____

Address _____

City _____ State/Zip _____